Lew

❧ AND ❧

Marcella

COMMON PEOPLE — UNCOMMON LIVES

by

Lew Linde

Linde Publishing Company

ISBN 0-9674573-1-9

Additional copies of *Lew and Marcella, Common People— Uncommon Lives* can be purchased from:

Just Thinking...Bookstore
1208 Vermillion Street
Hastings, MN 55033
phone: (651) 438-3696
fax: (651) 438-2871
www.justthinkingbookstore.com

The cost of the book is $10.00, plus $3.50 for shipping and handling. Please remember that half of the sales proceeds will go to the scholarship fund of the American Association of University Women, Hastings Chapter.

ACKNOWLEDGMENT

Over the years I have written my fair share of letters, memorandums, social histories, legal documents and a few short stories which I found mostly enjoyable. When writing the stories of Marcella and myself, I found it to be exciting and the fulfillment of a life long dream. By no means is the book a comprehensive account of our lives, but I have tried to include some of our significant memories and highlights.

Now a word of thanks to those people who made this venture successful. Paul, our son, a well known author, served as my editor. He has the ability to sharpen up ideas, facts, phrases and sentences. Son Ken and daughter, Sara proofread the manuscript. Kate Kelley, my competent typist was always cooperative and maintained a tight schedule.

A further word of thanks to those friends and relatives who provided valuable information and stories about Marcella. Special mention should be made of her sister, Rosie Sontag, friends Beth Kane, Helyn Duff and Fran Mlynarczyk.

Finally my gratitude to my wonderful children, Ken, Kay, Rick, Paul and Sara for their colorful vignettes and insights of our family.

This book is my gift to our family and friends.

—Lew Linde

PREFACE

Lew said keep it simple because that's his style. No muss, no fuss, no hyperbole. That's why the name of the book is "Common People, Uncommon Lives".

Although Lew Linde and Marcella Ruhr Schulzensohn Linde both came from white-collar families, they were also tied by time to generations of hardworking farmers; those who beat a living out of the ground of Minnesota and, before then, the turf of northern Europe. Their parents, Hermund and Inga Linde, and Ferdinand and Marie Ruhr, were still very much connected to the land.

A country doctor and his wife, known by her gentility and faith, threaded the fabric of both rural and small-town life in west central Minnesota, which Lew still refers to as "God's country". A small-town banker and his wife, known to be devout and exacting, weathered the Great Depression, riding out bumps of business that included making loans to farmers when times were lean.

Lew and Marcella are and were fundamentally full of piety, and, at the same time, pious. Their personalities developed in response to their forebears; by the members of the generations preceding them whom benefited from God's gift of bounty from not-always-fertile soil. I don't mean to denote "piety" and "pious" so much in the traditional religious sense, and I certainly don't intend it in the slightly pejorative way in which those words are sometimes used. I mean it in the way that Webster's Collegiate Dictionary defined it, among its alternate definitions—with piety meaning a "fidelity to natural obligations (as to parents)", and pious as "showing loyal reference for a person or thing".

In "Common People, Uncommon Lives", you will be reading the stories of two individuals, each of them unique, but together making a great team, one of whose tasks it was to raise those wild and wooly Linde kids, whose brief anecdotes, filtered by time, also appear in the book.

One story, Dad's biography of Mom, is full of pride and love, detailing the life and accomplishments of his wife. Her personal fortitude, caring nature, and obvious intellectual and interpersonal skills shine throughout the work.

The other story, Dad's autobiography, is not written out of a sense of hubris, but rather from the perspective of one who wants to get the stories out there, allowing his readers to know him through his personal history. His essentially gentle nature, humanitarianism, and goofy sense of humor are clearly present.

Common people—Mom and Dad were Midwestern products of the Great Depression—good listeners, industrious, pragmatic, not materialistic, not flashy; they came from a place of humility, where Mother Nature assisted God in the ruling of Heaven and Earth.

But, they lead and led uncommon lives, distinguished by their service to others, which is a road even less traveled these days by us members of the human race.

So, thank God for Lew and Marcella.

—Paul Linde

THIS BOOK IS DEDICATED TO

Marcella

TABLE OF CONTENTS

MARCELLA'S VALIANT FIGHT

The fall weather was unseasonably warm for October 26th, "short-sleeve weather", one might say. On that Saturday night Marcella and I were invited to attend the wedding of Diane Sheehy, a lawyer colleague of mine, at St. Andrew's Church in Mahtomedi. Everything about the wedding was perfect. The bride, as usual, was beautiful. A reception was held in the church afterwards where we had an opportunity to visit with mutual friends and their families.

Since it was an early evening wedding, we returned to our home mid-evening. Shortly after our arrival, Marcella said she wasn't feeling well, experiencing what seemed to her something like symptoms of the flu. Thinking a good night's rest would make her feel better, she went to bed before ten.

Through the years, Marcella had always been in excellent health and reluctant to seek medical help. So I sensed something was wrong when she woke me about five o'clock and told me, "Lew, I really feel sick, please take me to the emergency room."

The doctor on duty in the local ER early that Sunday morning examined her and conducted some routine tests. She concluded that Marcella was suffering from an infection of unknown origin. Marcella was given a generic antibiotic medicine to treat the infection and was told that her condition was not serious enough that an admission to the hospital would be required. The internist on call that morning was consulted for a second opinion and she decided that Marcella should be admitted to the hospital for further tests. Preliminary examinations revealed the possibilities of malignancies in her lower back and on the left side of her lungs. In the meantime, the flu-like symptoms persisted and an intravenous line for fluids and medicines was ordered.

Monday and Tuesday went by without any improvement in her condition. Marcella continued to suffer with abdominal pain, fatigue and low grade fever. The medical staff remained focused on the chest and abdominal masses. The doctors, first and foremost, felt that the masses needed to be treated. By Wednesday, the doctors were even more baffled and requested a transfer to United Hospital in St. Paul for further evaluations. Dr. John Carlson, a well-regarded general surgeon, who had not been consulted until Wednesday reviewed her case and examined Marcella. He diagnosed a ruptured appendix and advised Marcella that she needed surgery immediately.

Early that evening, Dr. Carlson spoke with Marcella while she was lying on the gurney and gave her even more bad news. He told Marcella that the infection had spread throughout her whole abdomen. Dr. Carlson also told her that her condition was so critical that during the surgery he may have to remove some of her large bowel and construct a colostomy. Marcella, who always greatly respected Dr. Carlson and his surgical skills, gave her consent to do whatever was necessary.

After our family waited for two hours in the visitor's room during the surgery, Dr. Carlson emerged from the operating room and said, rather excitedly and somewhat desperately, "when I opened Marcella up, pus shot all over." Dr. Carlson confirmed what we suspected—Marcella's appendix had been ruptured.

Marcella returned to her room after the surgery—somewhat groggy and loaded down with IV lines and tubes. These days, appendectomy incisions are usually less than a few inches long. In Marcella's case her incision ran the full length of her abdomen. The wound was left open to prevent a return of the infection. While the delay in proper diagnosis called the quality of her medical care into question, the nursing care was first-rate. Marcella was given morphine to hold back the pain. Unfortunately, this being Marcella's first experience with it, the morphine caused bad side effects. During the day things went quite smoothly, but as night fell, Marcella experienced confusion, anxiety and fearfulness. Paul, our doctor son, spent several nights with Marcella providing support and comfort.

During this ordeal, Marcella, true to her personality, did not complain about the multitude of her aches and pains. As did the family, Marcella wondered why the medical staff did not pay careful attention initially to her symptoms and missed the diagnosis. As her stay progressed, her room was adorned with many floral pieces. Likewise, the daily mail brought many get well cards.

One week after surgery Marcella was considered well enough to return home with the provision that visiting nurses would change her dressings and provide limited nursing care as needed. The medical staff confirmed that Marcella needed a further diagnostic evaluation to determine the nature and extent of her tumors. However, the incision had to fully heal before further tests could be done. After a wait of about six weeks, an appointment was made at the Oncology Clinic in St. Paul for early December.

After the series of blood tests, scans, and biopsies were completed, we had a consultation with her oncologist on December 17th. This proved to be a very difficult meeting for the doctor, Marcella and me. In as warm and comforting terms as possible, the doctor explained to Marcella that she had a neuroendrocine cancer. He stated that she had a rare form of cancer for which there was no known cure though the disease could be controlled for the time being by chemotherapy and radiation. In no uncertain terms, the doctor indicated that to forego treatment could bring about her demise in a matter of a few months. Marcella decided to begin chemotherapy.

On December 28th, Marcella began her chemotherapy treatments in St. Paul. During the next five months, she would need to receive chemotherapy for two consecutive days each month. Each day of treatment consisted of multiple medications given by intravenous line over several hours. The treatments took a physical toll on Marcella, causing severe side effects. Despite being given anti-nausea medications, Marcella would suffer with nausea, vomiting and fatigue for several days after the treatment. After a typical two-day session, her nausea and loss of appetite would result in an average weight loss of ten pounds. After the second treatment series, Marcella lost all of the hair on her head. With the help of Linda Tix, Marcella's favorite hair stylist, an attractive natural hair piece was obtained. During this time, Marcella wore several different head scarves as well.

With this significant change in her life, Marcella continued to display a calm, positive attitude about life. She was not one to feel sorry for herself. Each two-day session proved to be more difficult and tedious than the previous one. After her final treatment in May 1997, follow-up scans and examinations revealed no trace of tumors. Her doctor was pleased with the results, but also cautioned that Marcella was not out of the woods. Marcella was instructed to undergo periodic scans and blood tests to keep close tabs on the disease and the effects of the chemotherapy. All of Marcella's family and friends were very pleased that her condition had markedly improved.

With better health, Marcella resumed some of her previous activities such as Bridge Club every other Tuesday afternoon, one-hour adoration of the Blessed Sacrament at St. Elizabeth Ann Seton Catholic Church every Wednesday, helping patients attend mass at the Augustana Home once a month, and, of course, her usual rounds of family gatherings and monthly bridge playing with longtime friends, the Shimas, Krugers and Waldbilligs.

The routine scans and tests continued. Around the 4th of July, she developed numbness in her hands and feet, a complication of her previous chemotherapy treatments called a neuropathy. These symptoms proved to be more of a nuisance rather than an obstacle and it did not deter Marcella from enjoying many busy and fulfilling activities on a daily basis. That July we took an escorted ten-day bus trip to the western United States. We experienced the majestic beauty of Theodore Roosevelt National Park in North Dakota, Glacier and Yellowstone National Parks in Montana, the Grand Tetons in Wyoming, and, finally, Mount Rushmore in South Dakota. The trip was the fulfillment of our long-time dream to see those national treasures. Later that same month, Marcella and I traveled to San Francisco to spend a few days with Laurie and Paul. A highlight of this visit was a three day trip along the rugged northern Californian coast. We spent two nights in a cottage high on a bluff overlooking the Pacific Ocean. It was thrilling to watch those big breakers hit the shore.

In August, a scan revealed that a tumor had returned to the left side of her lung. Marcella's oncologist prescribed radiation treatments rather than another round of chemotherapy.

We made trips twice a week to St. Paul for these treatments. Thankfully, the radiation treatments caused few side effects. Marcella was able to continue most of her normal routines as she had in the past. These treatments were monitored closely by the radiation oncologist with various tests and particularly X-rays of the site being treated.

What a difference a year makes. One year earlier we had to cancel a trip to Branson, Missouri to see the stage & musical shows. In spite of the fact that Marcella was still having radiation treatment, her doctor gave her permission to make the Branson trip. We took in five shows that week. Marcella especially enjoyed the Andy Williams show. On the way to Branson, we stopped at the Precious Moments factory and store in Missouri. Marcella always liked their figurines.

Our family celebrated Thanksgiving at our home. For the Christmas season, we enjoyed traditional celebrations at our various family-homes. Marcella always loved the Christmas season and found joy in buying Christmas gifts for the family. She enjoyed the variety of Christmas tree ornaments that we hung on our real Christmas tree. This season was a blessing because once again the radiation therapy had worked.

Over the years Marcella and I had enjoyed escaping the Minnesota cold to visit Rosie and Ben at their winter home in Key Largo, Florida. In February we made another pleasurable journey to the Keys. The summer climate and the fine hospitality offered by Rosie and Ben made it a memorable event. A highlight was the day when Kay and Dave Ness and Mary and Chuck Anderson (Kay and Mary are first cousins of Rosie and Marcella) visited Key Largo. Reminiscing was the favored activity of the day while we all enjoyed a delicious lunch at an oceanside restaurant. We also took pleasure in playing games of bridge.

On May 1st, while I was working out in the backyard, Marcella rushed towards me and said that three young men were at the front door claiming that they were Lew's cousins from Norway. It was true. They each spoke passable English making communication easy. It was fun to hear about the Norway Linde relatives. They were our overnight guests and helped us celebrate our son Rick's 44th birthday at the Virginian restaurant.

In late June, our second cousin Leif Saele of Balestrand, Norway came for a two week visit. During that time we went to Moorhead, Minnesota to attend the dedication of the centuries old replica Hopperstad Stave Church, which is located in Vik, Norway. We stayed with my brother Erling and his wife Janice. Hilma (Lew's sister) and her husband, Russ, were also present. Needless to say, a great time was had by all.

After the Moorheard trip, Marcella began to experience bouts of nausea, irregular heartbeats, dehydration plus a poor appetite. As a result, she was hospitalized on July 21st and stomach ulcers were diagnosed. Four days later upon her discharge, Marcella left with prescriptions intended to treat ulcers and nausea. She saw her personal doctor the first part of August. Based upon the continuing tests and the examination, Dr. Larson's comments about Marcella's prognosis were rather guarded. It was at that point that the concept of eventual hospice care was mentioned.

In spite of Marcella's not feeling well with little or no appetite, her spirits were upbeat. She could have easily complained about herself, but she did not. Instead, Marcella continued to show her interest and affection in others, particularly her family. On August 17th the family gathered in Plymouth and spent the afternoon floating on pontoon boats on Medicine Lake near our son Rick's home. Despite the weather being hot and muggy, the event was happy and fun-filled.

Towards the end of August we saw Dr. Larson again and, in her opinion, Marcella was at the point where her illness could not be successfully treated. We were given the telephone number of a local Hospice Program. The Hospice staff explained that in order for a person to qualify for Hospice Care, two conditions had to be met: 1. a referral from the attending physician needed to verify that the patient was terminally ill, and 2. That the patient had six months or less to live. Marcella was not particularly alarmed at this prognosis and, consistent with her usual self, she accepted it with calmness. She knew that the disease would eventually catch up with her.

On September 4th we had an appointment with Marcella's oncologist in St. Paul. In his kind, gentle way he advised Marcella that she could either take chemotherapy pills which offered only a twenty percent chance of effectiveness, or let the disease run its course with help of Hospice Care. She was given a prescription in the event that she wanted more chemotherapy.

We were about seven miles south of St. Paul returning to Hastings when Marcella said "I don't believe further chemotherapy at this point will be of any more benefit, I'm going to let nature take its course".

After Marcella's decision, we went through the process of sharing the news with our family and friends. Despite their sadness about the situation, all members of our family fully supported her decision. On September 29th a representative from the Hospice Program came to the house to take Marcella's application and explained the program. I was designated as the caregiver. My responsibilities were mainly to make sure that Marcella's needs were fully met as her cancer took its natural course.

On October 1st, Sue Ostein, the nurse assigned by the Hospice Program made her initial call on Marcella. Sue explained her duties and responsibilities in the whole process. The main goal of hospice care was to keep Marcella as comfortable as possible. One of the main responsibilities of these nurses is taking full charge of the selection and administration of the medicines. While a patient's doctor does the prescribing, the nurse is given a wide range of discretion in managing the medicines.

In Marcella's case, her medicine regime was completely overhauled to better address her ongoing symptoms of nausea and pain. At first, the nurse visited about twice a week with the understanding that she would be available nearly any time. At the onset, Sue predicted that Marcella had two to four weeks to live. Marcella exceeded that prognosis, living another seven weeks.

From October 1st to October 31st Marcella was up everyday and able to take care of her basic needs. However, during this time, her appetite diminished considerably, she lost weight, and she developed general weakness. Her favorite foods were potato chips and Dairy Queen ice cream.

Once the word got out that Marcella's condition was on the wane, her family and friends made numerous visits. She very much enjoyed to reminisce. This was her way of saying a fond farewell to everyone. One day in my role as her designated caregiver, I felt that some visitors in Marcella's bedroom were staying too long so I politely suggested that perhaps they should end their visit. Marcella intervened and, in no uncertain terms said, "I'll decide when my visitors should leave." I never brought up the subject again.

Hospice Chaplain Father James Cassidy visited Marcella several times offering prayers, encouragement and the anointing service. On his first visit Marcella was just getting used to her situation and at one point the conversation turned to a subject that had nothing to do with her illness. Marcella believed that Catholic priests should be permitted to marry and that Catholic women be allowed to be priests. Father Cassidy did not disagree with her.

Another frequent and welcome visitor was Father Landelin Robling of St. Elizabeth Ann Seton. He called about every 3 or 4 days during the course of her illness. A typical call would include an anointing service for Marcella and those who happened to be home. His kindness, warmth, spiritual comfort, and, yes, his love were all inspiring and meaningful. Father Landelin demonstrated himself to be truly a man of God.

Paul and Laurie were in Hastings for about two weeks in October. Paul came back on November 7th. He was present until Marcella's death on November 21st. Paul's medical training was extremely helpful to the Hospice staff and Marcella.

When Marcella became totally bedfast on October 31, it was a major turning point in her final earthly journey. Her attitude and spirits were calm and peaceful. She never complained about fate and the fact that the end was near. Her thoughts were focused on her exit from this life—she had completely surrendered herself to God.

Over the years, Marcella was an excellent dresser and took pride in her appearance. One night in her bedroom in the presence of Kay and Sara, Marcella brought up the topic of what to wear for her funeral. Sara brought out several dresses and pantsuits from Marcella's closet and displayed them on the foot of the bed. None of them appealed to Marcella. She asked Kay to go shopping for something better. A few days later Kay brought three different outfits to show Marcella. After a short discussion, Marcella made her selection, a colorful blouse of blended fall colors and a pair of tan slacks which was typical of her good taste in clothing.

On another evening, at one of our family bedside conferences, Marcella stated her wishes for her funeral. With pencil and paper in hand, Ken listed Marcella's requests: that all of her nephews (7) to serve as pallbearers; that Gordon Gathright, with his powerful tenor voice sing "How Great Thou Art," "Ave Maria", and "The Lord's Prayer"; and that the 23rd Psalm be read or sang. Marcella also specified that all of the flowers at her visitation should be placed around the altar at her funeral at Saint Elizabeth Ann Seton. All of her wishes were honored.

About ten days before her demise, Marcella talked about contents of her obituary in the newspapers and admonished me not to forget to mention Don's name (her former husband) in the papers. The obituaries were completed.

During the last ten days, Father Landelin called almost every day. His prayers and words of comfort meant so much to Marcella and the family. Marcella mentioned that she experienced dreams in which she met Gert Payne, her deceased childhood friend, and her beloved late father Ferdinand Ruhr. The experiences lend truth to the concept that departed loved ones in Heaven are planning the triumphal entry of a loved one into Heaven.

Realizing that Marcella's physical condition was in decline and knowing that her days on earth were numbered, a Hospice Nurse came to provide overnight care in the evenings of November 19th and 20th. On that final night, I slept in the den and woke up at 4:00 a.m. The kind nurse was sitting in the living room and I asked how Marcella was faring. She replied that Marcella would not make it through the night, but that she would wake me a half hour before she thought Marcella would expire. At 6:15 a.m. she woke me and I summoned Paul and Sara. We all stood at Marcella's bedside and watched her take her last breath. Sara and I went over to Marcella, kissed her, said we loved her and said goodbye. It is said that a person's hearing is the last sense a dying person loses. Paul took advantage of this fact and said in a fond manner, "Mom, I'm so glad that your spirit is finally leaving your body, say hello to St. Peter for me". Marcella died at 6:44 a.m. on November 21st.

November 24th, the day of the funeral, the temperature was brisk and the sky was bright and sunny.

It was the kind of weather that Marcella had wished for on her funeral day. With a choir of 40 voices, three priests, many friends and relatives, it was exactly the kind of funeral Marcella had planned. Bob Caturia told people later that it was one of the most beautiful funerals he had ever conducted.

Eulogy for Marcella Linde—November 24, 1998— Given by Ken Linde

(This is not intended to be word for word. It is my best recollection of what I said. I used only a sheet of key words and phrases for the actual delivery of the eulogy.)

(Greetings and Thanks to all.)

It is tough to follow that song. (On Eagle's Wings) But we all know that He really does lift us up on eagle's wings and He does hold us in the palm of His hand.

Perhaps some of you also have a flip calendar of

scriptures in your home. Carol and I look at this (held up the calendar) every morning and today's scripture is so appropriate for this day—Revelation 21:4—"He will wipe every tear from their eyes. There will be no more death or mourning or crying or pain, for the old order of things has passed away."

Let me tell you about my sisters and brothers.

Kay—loving, unconditionally and sacrificially. Kay would do whatever she had to do for her two children— so that they could become all that they are gifted to be. Often preferring others over herself.

Rick—conscientious, honest, caring, insightful, funny, true to God, himself and to his family and friends. A family man without his own kids—"I love my nieces to pieces". Generous in giving of himself and his money.

Paul—intelligent, insightful, a professional listening ear with a humane caring heart. Funny, sometimes off the wall. His high school football nickname was Mad-Dog. Makes people feel comfortable with him—no pretenses or false airs.

Sara—a teacher who loves kids and is a wonderful example to them. A good and true friend. Talkative, loves to talk on the phone. Funny. Has a sense of compassion and care for the underdog. Tends to look for the good in others. Encouraging.

And then there is me. Enough said!

Right about now, Mom would be saying to the

person next to her—"That was different!" (Probably only our family will get this inside joke.)

So, why during this eulogy for my mother have I told you about my sisters and brothers? I have just painted a picture of Mom—Marcella. The qualities that you and others see in us, are the qualities instilled in us by her daily and diligent example of living. We are who we are because of who she was. In a sense, she lives on in her family. She lives on in more than just our memories.

Mom was generous, caring, talkative, insightful, humorous, accepting, encouraging, and above all, loving. I think I can speak for my brothers and sisters when I say that we have never known a day where we didn't know that Mom loved us very much. Even in her last weeks, she had something encouraging and welcoming to say to each of us. Throughout her life she needed us to know she loved us. Toward the end, when she could barely speak, Mom would say "I love you" to us as we left her room.

Mom tended to handle the big things much better than the small things. That is a trait we also picked up from her! As things have happened in our family over the years, Mom handled the big issues, the traumatic issues, more easily than things like Dad bringing the wrong item home from the store. I think it goes back to 1955, when at the age of 30 and with three children under age 4, her husband Donald Schulzensohn died. She had to learn very quickly that if you're not careful and watchful, the big things of life will consume you. Overnight, she became Mom, Dad, homemaker and breadwinner to me, Kay and Rick. It seems from that day forward, she could more easily handle the larger issues of life.

Or maybe it was because Mom had been trained to lead, solve problems and administer. After graduating from the College of St. Catherine with a nursing degree, she became the hospital administrator and head of nurses at the age of 25. Quite a feat in the early 50s—actually, quite a feat today as well.

About 2 years after Don's death, a new man came into Mom's life and into ours as well. Lew Linde took for himself a wife and her wedding gift to him was three children. He gave us some spelling relief when he adopted us and gave us his surname (12 letters in Schulzensohn to just 5 in Linde) and joined mom in our upbringing, our education, and ventures into life. Along the way God blessed Mom and Dad's union with two children—Paul and Sara.

My brothers, sisters and I all learned to have a sense of duty or responsibility to give back to society and to those around us. Mom was a generous volunteer—both with her time and her resources. Some of you here may remember her as a perennial election judge—others may have worked with Mom at the immunization clinic or the bloodmobile—and one of her real loves was giving her time to Birthright. I can easily tell you these things all day—and I should because I'm her son. But I want to let two cards that Mom received her last two weeks speak for her.

One lady wrote, "I was thinking one day how in June 1988 when I moved to Hastings as a new widow and I called the phone number in the Hastings paper to see if I could work in the canteen at the bloodmobile. How very happy I was to meet you, Marcella. I was alone and so lonely and you remembered me each time I came to help and I was so drawn to you. I thank God for you and your caring."

Another friend wrote, "Marcella, you were always so positive about all that happened at the immunization clinic. You brought us all your wisdom and your sense of humor. You were a role model for me—as one who gained joy in giving. Your friendship has been a deep treasure, and our memories are golden."

One day when Father Landelin came to visit Mom, he told a story. Though I wasn't there at the time, some who were thought it a bit strange that Father would tell a story about a man dying of cancer to a woman dying of cancer. But when he finished, all knew the meaning and purpose of him telling it. The story goes like this— a man dying of cancer is asked by his priest, "Do you have any last wishes about your burial?" The man replied that he wanted to be buried with his Bible in one hand and a fork in the other. The priest was somewhat surprised at this. He said, "I understand wanting to be buried with a Bible, but not a fork!!" The dying man said, "Well, you remember all those church suppers we have had? The ladies always tell you to keep your fork. And then I know there is something better coming.

And of course we believe there is something better ahead for Mom and for all of us. The gospel account from John 14 on the front of the program reveals what we base our belief on—the words of Jesus telling us that He goes to prepare a place for us and that He will return to take us to that place. Mom knew that Jesus alone is the way, the truth and the life, and that no one comes to the Father but through Jesus.

Mom surely loved and honored God and we were raised to have a faith in God. After Mom was diagnosed with cancer in December of 1996, we along with many others prayed diligently for her healing. And in fact, after chemotherapy, Mom was cancer free for about 6 months. But the cancer came back. We all prayed more. We prayed for a miracle. But God didn't give us one—instead He gave us many.

He allowed us to get a glimpse of how one of His precious children could obtain a peace and acceptance of her own death. He allowed Mom to have a resurgence at which time we talked and joked and played cards together. Mom even ate a little bit at this time. He allowed Mom to be able to talk about and plan her own funeral—she chose the scriptures and songs for today's celebration. And finally, He chose to give Mom the ultimate healing—eternal peace and life with Himself in Heaven.

After her death as we kids talked about Mom and her life, we were reminded of several versus from Proverbs 31. I will read verses 25 through 31.

"Strength and dignity are her clothing, And she smiles at the future. She opens her mouth in wisdom, And the teaching of kindness is on her tongue. She looks well to the ways of her family, And she does not eat the breath of idleness. Her children rise up and bless her; Her husband also, and he praises her, saying: "Many daughters have done nobly, But you excel them all." Charm is deceitful and beauty is vain, But a woman who fears the Lord, she shall be praised. Give her the product of her hands, And let her works praise her in the gates."

Amen.

The service ended in song. Marcella was buried that fall day in a plot marked with a headstone that reads "Takk for alt". And so we say to Marcella, thanks for everything.

Marcella

THE ROSEMOUNT YEARS

Marcella was born late on a Monday evening, March 16, 1925, in the midst of the "Roaring Twenties". She was the youngest of three children, with her brother Joe being the oldest and sister Rosie coming next. Since Rosemount was mostly a purely Irish community, some people, even Marcella's parents hoped, that she would have been born on St. Patrick's Day. In spite of Marcella's complete German ancestry, many people thought she was Irish because of her many freckles, reddish-brown wavy hair and her natural beauty.

Marcella's dad, Ferdinand, was the president and owner of the Rosemount National Bank. The family's financial status was above average, though reliable sources indicate that the Ruhrs lived very modest lives. The only exception to this rule is that they took two-week summer vacations while most folks had to be content with staying at home during the Depression era.

In the fall of 1930, at the age of five, Marcella entered her first year of schooling. Her first grade teacher and friend of the family was Dorothy Therstein. Rosemount did not have a Kindergarten. Marcella's parents believed that she had the intelligence and ability to succeed. They were proven right as Marcella always earned excellent grades throughout her education and was an honor student in her high school class.

Throughout her entire life, Marcella enjoyed a warm and loving relationship with her sister Rosie despite their difference of five years. Until Rosie went off to College, they played with dolls and read books together, and even shared the same double bed. With her warm, friendly manner, Marcella easily developed close friendships with several neighborhood girls. In her growing years Marcella's close companion and playmate was Gert Bernier. Her father was the local auto dealer. Marcella and Gert enjoyed riding their bikes around Rosemount. The neighborhood girls' playhouse was situated in the old chicken coop in Ruhr's backyard. This particular group of friends grew up together and stayed in touch with each other. They eventually formed the "Birthday Club" which is still in existence now except that two members have gone on to that Great Birthday Club in the sky. This lifelong group of friends included Marcella, Gert Bernier, Helyn Bartel, Mary Eva McDonald, Sally McDonald, Jeanne McMenomy, Mary Chapdelaine, and Eileen O'Leary.

Marcella entered high school in the 9th grade in 1938. Besides taking the traditional classes, she played coronet in the high school band. Rosie on the clarinet and Joe on the saxaphone preceded Marcella in the Rosemount High School Band. The school did not have a regular band teacher, but hired a part-time director, Mr. Whittbecker of Minneapolis. In addition to performing at school functions, the band performed outdoor concerts in the Rosemount Community Square on summer Saturday nights. The band also played at band festivals in other communities. Marcella enjoyed playing in the band with the notable exception of their annual march in the St. Paul Winter Carnival. Imagine playing a brass instrument outdoors in the wintertime while wearing band uniforms that failed to keep a person warm.

High school days were happy days for Marcella. With a gifted intelligence, it was rather easy for her to maintain high grades. She wanted to enter the nursing profession as long as she could remember. In high school she took all of the science courses that were offered—in preparation for college. At the time classes in Latin were a prerequisite for nursing. Interestingly enough, it was later discovered that knowledge of Latin was not that important for those working in the health profession. Marcella always said that Latin did help her ability to spell, understand word origins and sound out words.

Marcella always regreted that high school sports were closed to girls. Cheerleading for the boys teams was the closest that Marcella got to high school sports. Marcella loved to dance. While Rosemount did not host a youth recreational center, Al's Café, a local restaurant and gathering place, had a juke box and a dance floor. Marcella and her friends spent many free hours dancing at Al's. They also attended dances at Coates, Spring Lake Park, Hastings, Farmington and other neighboring farm towns.

In 1942, when Marcella was a senior, a Popularity Poll which included several different categories was conducted for the entire high school. Included, were "most talented", "hardest-working boy", "best boy dancer", "smartest student" and so on. Marcella won in three categories—"Prettiest Girl", "Friendliest Person" and "Most Popular Girl". Marcella's true, friendly and warm personality came through to all her fellow students.

Mention should be made of her close personal relationships with Alan O'Rourke and Edward Tousignant. Alan and Marcella were classmates from the first grade through high school. Their mothers always shared the common belief that Alan and Marcella would make an ideal married couple. A farmer's son, Alan, was good looking and very bright. He was the valedictorian of his class. They were always close friends, but never sweethearts. Alan went on to get a college degree and eventually settled in Colorado.

Edward or "Eddie" as some called him was a couple of years older than Marcella. He came from a large farm family. He was handsome, with a pleasant personality. Marcella and Eddie went together during some of Marcella's high school and college years. Marcella later said that she saw many positive things in Eddie, but could not see herself as a farmer's wife.

ROSEMOUNT HIGH SCHOOL
GRADUATION CLASS OF 1942

Rosemount Class Roll Is Twenty-five

The commencement program at Rosemount will be Friday, May 29th, at the Rosemount high school this year when twenty-five seniors will be graduated. The commencement speaker will be Andrew L. Olson.

The valedictorian is Allen O'Rourke and the salutatorian is Phyllis Schwanz. Other awards are: Phyllis Schwanz and Marvin Rahn, citizenship: Alvera Ratzlaff and Francis McDonough, music and athletics.

The class officers are: George Helling, president; Muriel Perron, vice president; Marvin Rahn, secretary; Francis McDonough, treasurer. The complete program is:

COMMENCEMENT

Processional, "Pomp and Circumstance" by Elgar, played by the Rosemount High School band.

Invocation, Rev. J. H. Kolberg.

"Gallaway Piper" by Treharne, sung by the Girls' Sextet.

Salutatory address, Phyllis Schwanz.

"Whispering Leaves, by Weidt, played by the Rosemount school band.

Valedictory address, Allen O'Rourke.

Vocal solo by Katherine Baumgartner, accompanied by Olive Nietfeld.

Commencement address by Andrew L. Olson.

Presentation of the class, Supt. L. G. Baumgartner.

Presentation of diplomas, Hubert Geraghty.

Whistling solo, "Indian Love Call" by Katherine Baumgartner, accompanied by Olive Nietfeld.

"God Bless America", audience.

Benediction, Rev. J. H. Kolberg.

Recessional, "March Mutual" by Bennet, played by the Rosemount High School band.

Article taken from Dakota County Tribune—May 22, 1942.

Marcella was awarded a four year scholarship to the College of St. Catherine to study nursing.

*Marcella's graduation picture from the
College of St. Catherine's, 1946.*

TRAINING TO BE A NURSE

In the fall of 1942, when the United States was involved in a global nightmare otherwise known as World War II, Marcella began her nurse's training at the College of St. Catherine. The United States was in a true crisis situation—fighting a war simultaneously in Western Europe and the Pacific. Many of Marcella's boy classmates either were drafted or enlisted in the Armed Forces. The DuPont Corporation was in the process of building a factory in Rosemount to produce smokeless gunpowder. Everything in our society was geared to the war effort. For example, rationing of gasoline, tires, sugar, butter, meat, and shoes was in full motion.

Marcella enrolled in the five-year nursing course that would lead to a Bachelor of Science degree as a registered nurse. From the fall of 1942 until the summer of 1944, Marcella lived on campus and took pre-nursing classes full-time. Not only did she take the customary classes of biology, chemistry, physics, but also classes in psychology, sociology, philosophy, and religion. Of note, the future wife of Senator Eugene McCarthy was her English professor.

During this time Marcella lived in the dormitories of Whitby Hall and Ceceline Hall where the discipline was rather rigorous. The rules included strict enforcement of designated study hours, no smoking and quiet times. Whenever the students left the dormitory to go anywhere it was mandatory for them to wear a skirt, hat, gloves and silk stockings. Heaven forbid that they should be caught wearing anklets. Due to the war, nylons and silk stockings were next to impossible to secure. To overcome this shortage, students painted their legs a stocking color, even in the dead of winter.

Since almost all of the single men were off in the military service, dating opportunities were limited. At dances the ratio of women to men was 10 to 1. Since smoking in the dormitories was forbidden, the students would go to a local convenience store for a smoke and a coke. Going to the movies was a favorite pastime and attending sporting events such as swimming and volleyball was a popular option. Fran Mlynarczyk, a roommate and classmate of Marcella, reported how all of her classmates liked Marcella and considered her a "friend for life". Marcella was not one to gossip or badmouth others. In spite of the fact that Marcella came from a family of means, she never flaunted her family's wealth.

While Marcella was generally in excellent terms with her parents, a rather serious disagreement broke out between them in the spring of 1943. The United States was engaged in a war that threatened its own existence. Trained nurses were surely needed to enter the military service. U.S. Army nurse recruiters were present on campus to enlist nursing students in the Cadet Nurse Corps, and since enlisting meant that Marcella would enter the military service after graduation, the Ruhrs strongly opposed her idea to join the Cadet Nurse Corps. They held the realistic fear that she would become a war victim.

Reluctantly, they gave Marcella their blessing to join the Corps. Amazingly, all of Marcella's 30 classmates joined the Corps. Each student had to sign a contract which provided that—in exchange for full tuition and books, board and room, uniforms and fifty dollars per month in wages—they would agree to spend a minimum of one year in the military after successfully completing their training. The uniforms issued were in the basic color of navy blue. Their wardrobe included two skirts, a three quarter length blue cape, two blazers, berets, blouses, nurses uniforms, an overcoat, work shoes, black pumps and dresses. The summer uniforms consisted of blue/white seer sucker dresses with a military hat.

The new quasi-military status did enhance Marcella's and her fellow students' social lives. In their uniforms they could go to U.S.O. clubs and secure the same amenities that servicemen received. Included in these benefits were free cigarettes, refreshments and movie tickets. By assuming this status, it represented their willingness to serve in the war effort.

Fortunately for Marcella, once the war ended, the requirement of entering the military at the completion of their training was dropped. Furthermore, wearing the uniform was no longer mandatory, but her educational expenses continued to be paid by the government.

After two years of college studies, Marcella moved from campus to the student nurses' quarters at St. Joseph Hospital where she began full time nurses' training until she graduated in June of 1946.

The training was rigorous. It included six eight-hour days working "on the floor", which meant bathing, feeding and giving medications to patients. Marcella became an expert on how to make hospital beds. The working hours were eight-hour shifts—around the clock, seven days a week, and 365 days a year. Besides completing classes of the nursing profession, they also returned to campus for their regular classes. Even if they had worked all night, they were expected to attend all classes.

Marcella's training was generic in nature, so in the summer of 1945, she was placed on a rotation in which she lived at Ancker Hospital (now Regions Hospital) in St. Paul. Her class was assigned to work exclusively with hospitalized polio patients. History tells us that the year of 1945 was the height of the national polio epidemic. People of all ages were either dying or becoming paralyzed from this dreaded disease. Classmate Beth Hunter Kane related that all of the students worked six-day weeks. Their main instructor, Birgit Tofte, was an excellent teacher, but also a tough taskmaster. Legend has it that one day, while Miss Tofte had her uniformed class lined up for a personal inspection, one of the students passed out and fell to the floor. Paying no attention to the downed student, she admonished class members to leave the unconscious classmate alone; Miss Tofte stated in no uncertain terms that she will have to wake up on her own. Marcella's work was hazardous, because polio was a particularly contagious disease and careful sanitary measures had to be taken in dealing with the patients. On this rotation Marcella had the chance to observe and work with the world-famous Australian nurse Sister Elizabeth Kenny. It was Sister Kenny who introduced new procedures in treating polio patients, which incorporated hot packs and hot towels, among other things.

In the fall of 1945 Marcella served a three-month rotation in psychiatric nursing at the Fergus Falls State Hospital. This rural hospital housed about one thousand patients with a wide variety of mental illness diagnoses. Since this was the era before psychotropic drugs, electro- and insulin-shock treatments were widely used. The straightjacket was a commonly used remedy to control agitated patients.

The hospital's medical director, Dr. Patterson, had the reputation of being a very humane and caring professional.

He always dressed casually and quietly was known to visit patients on the wards at almost any hour. Mary Weber Hagen, a nursing student at the time, tells a story that typifies Dr. Patterson's casual demeanor. One day, late in the afternoon she saw a man walking in one of the hospital tunnels with a dog. He was dressed in ordinary clothes and did not seem to be headed in any one direction. Mary, following hospital procedures, firmly advised him that he should immediately return to his ward. It was then that Mary formally met Dr. Patterson.

In those days medical doctors reigned supreme. They sometimes wanted to be treated with inordinate respect. Marcella, with her naturally friendly manner, did well with medical doctors. For the most part, they respected her. However, a well known surgeon, whose name will not be mentioned, sometimes acted like he was in a harem, as he freely pinched and touched the bottoms of uniformed nurses. Unfortunately, a complaint by a nurse to higher authorities would go nowhere.

Through it all Marcella successfully completed her nurses' training with a Bachelor of Science degree from the College of St. Catherine on June 6, 1946.

1946—1955 Years Of Hope, Happiness And Sadness

Marcella graduated from the College of St. Catherine on June 6, 1946 with a Bachelor of Science degree, following an arduous four years and a sometimes tedious nurses' training. Afterward she passed the state board examination in nursing to become a bona fide R.N., Registered Nurse. Because of her talent, training ability and intelligence, Marcella was offered and accepted the position of Assistant Supervisor in the department of pediatrics at St. Joseph's Hospital.

At the time, a polio epidemic was raging in Minnesota and other parts of the country. During World War II, the Du Pont Corporation built a large plant a few miles east of Rosemount to manufacture smokeless gun powder. Since the war ended before the plant started production, the building stood empty, never used for its original purpose. Because the University of Minnesota Hospitals in Minneapolis were inundated with polio victims during this time, they needed more space. The University converted the vacant and unused defense plant offices into a rehabilitation center for its polio patients, who were stricken with muscle weakness and paralysis and required a rigorous regimen of physical therapy and rehabilitation to recover fromg the illness.

The following Pioneer Press article of December 6, 1946 tells a story of Marcella's work at this facility:

By NEWELL H. BARNARD
Staff Writer

ROSEMOUNT, MINN—Miss Marcella Ruhr, 21 years old, daughter of Mr. and Mrs. F. A. Ruhr of Rosemount, has been named superintendent of the University of Minnnesota Polio hospital at Rosemount . She joined the nursing staff of the hospital Sept. 15 and was elevated to her present position on Dec. 1. She also holds the office of nursing supervisor.

In 1946 Miss Ruhr was graduated from the College of St. Catherine with a Bachelor of Science degree and obtained her hospital training at St. Joseph's in St. Paul. After graduation at St. Joseph's she continued at the hospital as assistant supervisor in pediatrics. She held this position until joining the university staff.

As superintendent of the hospital together with the office of nursing supervisor, Miss Ruhr has a full-time schedule. The personnel of the hospital numbers 40 and in addition to eight regular nurses includes nurses aides, physiotherapists, kitchen workers and janitors. Resident physician and co-worker with Miss Ruhr is Dr. A. Feinstein.

The hospital observed its first anniversary Friday.

At present there are 54 patients ranging from 2 to

37 years old. Of these, 36 are Minnesota victims of the 1946 outbreak, including three from Minneapolis. There are three out-of-state 1946 victims. Remainder of the patients are from previous epidemics or isolated cases of past years.

Perhaps the outstanding case the hospital is now dealing with, according to Miss Ruhr, is that of a 37-year-old patient, Miss Helen Huper of Alden, Minnesota. For 22 years she has managed to get around by the use of heavy braces and with the aid of "sticks".

Throughout those years she believed she was beyond any help. A few months ago she learned of the polio hospital and entered the university clinic. On Nov. 14 was admitted to the polio hospital for physiotherapy treatments. Since that time her progress has been remarkable. Asked, if she could now stand without her braces she quickly replied, "Stand, I can now walk a little without them."

The Rosemount branch of the University of Minnesota Hospital ceased operations in the summer of 1947, after which Marcella accepted the position of supervisor of the St. Joseph Hospital's Department of Pediatrics. On August 12, 1947 Marcella's niece, the first born daughter of Marcella's sister Rosie and her husband Ben Sontag, was born at St. Joseph's.

Marcella's next significant move in life occurred in the summer of 1948 when she was hired as the Administrator of the hospital in Rush City, Minnesota. Marcella liked to tell the story about her interview with the hospital's board. On a warm and cloudless day, Marcella and her mother, Marie, drove to Rush City for the interview. It wasn't until they arrived in Rush City that Marie insisted that she sit in with Marcella during the interview. Marie's rationale for being present was that she wanted to tell the board all of the wonderful things and the many accomplishments of Marcella. She thought that Marcella was too modest about herself. Marcella finally won the argument to go before the board herself. Marie reluctantly waited in the city park. Marcella must have passed the interview with flying colors because she got the job. She was the overall administrator of the hospital in Rush City until June 15, 1950.

From the professional and personal point of view, Marcella's time in Rush City had to be one of the most important parts of her life. This is when and where she met Don Schulzensohn, her first husband. As you will note in the newspaper article from the Rush City Post, dated June 16, 1950, the Rush City Hospital harbored a medical bee hive. Marcella kept a watchful eye over all of the medical activities in addition to fulfilling various administrative duties such as supervising the nursing staff and housekeepers, meeting sales people and relating to the hospital's physicians.

No mater when a genuine medical emergency happened—whether it was nights, weekends or holidays—Marcella was summoned to oversee the process of evaluation and treatment. Because Rush City was on Highway 61, the hospitals emergency room received many victims of horrible automobile accidents. As a firm believer in Christian infant baptism, Marcella sometimes baptized critically ill babies in the hospital when it was apparent that a baby would not live long after birth.

The following article appeared in the Rush City Post on June 16, 1950. It gives an account of the history and activities of the hospital:

Miss B. Sorkness
New Administrator
At Local Hospital

June 15th is a special day at the Rush City Hospital when the staff welcomes the new administrator, Miss Beatrice E. Sorkness and bids farewell to Miss Marcella Ruhr, who goes to Rosemount, Minnesota to prepare for her marriage to Donald Schulzensohn, on July the 8th.

The Rush City Hospital has been in operation a little over nine years. It was on May 14, 1941, when the first bed patient, Miss Myrtle Danielson, Harris, Minn., was registered.

On the 14th of June, 1950, the 9,233rd patient was admitted to the hospital, making an average of one thousand patients cared for each year. These figures are for bed patients, the OUT Patient figures run in to many more thousands.

The first baby born in the hospital was on May 17th, 1941, to Mr. and Mrs. Prosper Nys of Rush City. Mrs. Nys is on the staff of the hospital at this time. The first set of twins came on June 5th and 6th, 1941, baby daughters of Mr. and Mrs. F. Howard Lindall, Duluth, Minn.

On June 14th, 1950, there had been 1,834 prospective mothers admitted to the hospital. Among this group were several sets of twins so the number of new born babies would be slightly higher than the number of mothers.

The Rush City hospital, municipally owned is a 25 bed hospital equipped for general nursing care, maternity cases, X-ray and Laboratory work. It has a staff of 14 nurses, five house keepers, one bookkeeper, and one general utility man.

The net worth of the hospital as of December 31, 1949, was $89,537.23. The village was originally bonded $20,000 for the hospital and $5,000 has been paid on this debt. Regular payments are now being made on this obligation. The Board of Directors announced that $2,000 has been repaid to the Village Council on the $6,000 borrowed in November, 1949. It is expected this balance will be repaid in full during the current year.

During the past few weeks many social affairs have been held in honor of Miss Ruhr and her approaching marriage. The hospital staff congratulates Miss Ruhr and wishes Miss Sorkness the best of luck.

Marcella, with her physical attractiveness and friendly personality, never lacked for men asking her out. During her time in Rush City, Marcella began a courtship with Don Schulzensohn—one that developed into their engagement and subsequent marriage. After World War II, Don spent 18 months in the U.S. Army. He then took a job with the Minnesota Department of Natural Resources as a surveyor. Don possessed experience and training as an industrial lens maker, learning the trade from his father Oswald and through additional coursework at the Illinois Institute of Technology. After their marriage on July 8, 1950, Marcella and Don moved to Chicago where he pursued his craft in the same company in which his dad worked.

The best way to describe their wedding is to print the story from the Dakota County Tribune, which was printed on July 17, 1950.

RUHR-SCHULZENSOHN

Miss Marcella Ruhr—daughter of Mr. and Mrs. F. A. Ruhr of Rosemount, and Mr. Donald Schulzensohn, son of Mr. Oswald Schulzensohn and the late Mrs. Schulzensohn of Chicago, were married at 9 a.m., Saturday, July 8th in the Church of St. Joseph, Rosemount. Rev. James Furey officiated the double ring ceremony and nuptial mass. The church was beautifully decorated with flowers and lighted candelabra.

Mrs. Lee Dooley, a friend of the bride, sang, On This Day O Beautiful Mother, Panis Angelious, Ave Maria and O Lord I Am Not Worthy, accompanied by Mary Jean Corrigan at the organ.

The bride, who was given in marriage by her father, wore a bridal gown of net with floral embroidery of forget-me-nots over satin fashioned with a long court train. The gown had fitted bodice with net off-the-shoulder yolk edged with shirring, two panels of shirring extended from the waist to the bottom of the skirt. The long tight sleeves ended in a point over the wrist. She wore a fingertip veil of bridal illusion caught in to a lace bonnet, which was also worn by her sister, Mrs. Sontag, at her wedding. The bride carried a white prayerbook centered with an orchid and showers of stephanotis on satin streamers. Her only jewelry was a rhinestone necklace, a gift of the groom.

Mrs. Rosemarie Sontag of Hastings, was her sister's matron of honor. Her gown of yellow marquisette was fashioned similar to the bride's. She carried a colonial bouquet of yellow roses and lilac sweepeas.

The bridesmaid, Miss Sally McDonald of St. Paul,

From left to right: Ferdinand Ruhr, Marie Ruhr, Marcella,
Don Schulzensohn, Oswald Schulzensohn.

a close friend of the bride, wore a lilac gown identical
to Mrs. Sontag's. She carried a colonial bouquet of yellow roses and lilac sweetpeas. Both attendants wore ti-
aras and Santlots matching their gowns. Their jewelry
was rhinestone chokers and earrings, gifts of the bride.

The bride's niece, little Lynn Marie Sontag, was her
flower girl, wearing a floor length pale green frock with
a white hair ribbon. She carried a tiny colonial bouquet
of pink and white carnations.

The groom's attendants were Arthur Klein, Jr., of St.
Paul, a close friend of the groom's, as best man. Richard Lofstuen of Rush City, was groomsman. The ushers

were Benjamin Sontag of Hastings and Ralph Lofstuen of Rush City. The gentlemen of the wedding party were attired in black trousers and white dinner jackets with black bow ties and white carnations boutonnieres.

For her daughter's wedding, Mrs. Ruhr wore a teal blue dress trimmed with lace and white accessories. Her corsage was of pink and white tea roses.

A reception following the ceremony was held at the home of the bride's parents. The bridal table was centered with a three tier wedding cake and lighted candelabra. The reception hostesses were friends of the bride.

The wedding dinner for this bridal party and the immediate families was served at the West Twins in St. Paul at 8 p.m.

After a short honeymoon, the couple will be at home at 1442 Belle Plaine Avenue, Chicago, Illionois. For travel the bride wore a silk print dress with white accessories and wore an orchid corsage.

In the early years of their marriage until Don's untimely death in 1955, Marcella was extremely busy raising a family. Before Ken was born, Marcella worked as a nurse in a private hospital in Chicago. Unfortunately, Don was stricken with an active case of tuberculosis that caused him to be hospitalized for nine months in a sanitarium.

In spite of Don's illness, Marcella and Don were able to return to Minnesota for a vacation and to visit family and friends. After each of Marcella's and Don's children were born, the Ruhrs spent time in Chicago helping out Marcella.

Marcella was optimistic that Don would find a complete cure for his TB. As a part of the treatment for TB in those days, one of his lungs was medically collapsed. His cause of death came about when he developed pneumonia in the other healthy lung. Death came suddenly and unexpectedly. When Marcella returned to Minnesota and spoke with medical experts about Don's condition and death, she was informed that the treatment of Don's condition was outmoded. If he were treated in Minnesota at the time, the outcome may have been different.

The obituary from the Hastings Gazette of September 15, 1955:

Schulzensohn Rites At St. Boniface Church On September 6

Donald E. Schulzensohn of Arlington Heights, a surburb of Chicago, passed away September 1st, 1955 at St. Joseph's Hospital, Elgin, Ill., following a four day illness.

Vigil was held at the Geo. Alt Funeral Home in Chicago on Saturday, September 3rd and at the Caturia and Gahnz Funeral Home in Hastings on Monday, September 5th. Funeral services were conducted Tuesday, September 6th at 10 o'clock A. M. at St. Boniface church in Hastings with Rev. Father Lambert O. S. B., officiating at a requiem high mass. Interment was made in the church cemetery.

The palbearers were Arthur Klein, Jr., of St. Paul, Darcy Moses of Granite Falls, James Gluth of Rush City, Richard Lofstuen of Minneapolis, Eugene McDonald of St. Paul and William Quigley of Rosemount.

Mr. Schulzensohn was born in Chicago on January 23rd, 1928, the son of Oswald and the late Ilse Schulzensohn, later the family moved to Minneapolis where his mother passed away, he later made his home in Rush City where he graduated from high school and served in the U.S. army during World War II.

Upon his discharge from the army he was employed by the State of Minnesota as a surveyor in the conservation department. In May 1950 he accepted a position with Schneider-Cogswell Inc., in Chicago in optical engineering and furthered his education at the Illinois Institute of Technology becoming a quality control engineer, a position held at the time of his death.

On July 8th, 1950 Mr. Schulzensohn was united in marriage with Marcella Ruhr of Rosemount at St. Joseph's Church in Rosemount. Surviving besides his wife are two sons, Kenneth and Richard, one daughter, Kay Marie, parents, Oswald and Mary Schulzensohn of Chicago and a sister, Mrs. Gilda Murray of Dallas, Texas. Mr. Schulzensohn was a devoted husband and father and will be sadly missed by his family, relatives and many friends.

Attending the rites were relative and friends from Minneapolis, St. Paul, Chicago, Red Wing, Hastings, Cannon Falls, Osseo, Granite Falls, Lake City, Forest Lake, Rush City, Hampton, Farmington, Rosemount, Miesville, St. Croix Falls, Wis., Hudson, Wis., and Dallas, Texas.

To add tragedy upon tragedy, at the time of Don's death, the family of five had lived in a new home for only a few weeks in Arlington Heights, a suburb north of Chicago. Because of Don's untimely death, Marcella and the children moved to Hastings to be close to her parents in Rosemount and sister in Hastings.

Lew

THE EARLY YEARS 1928–1949

The memory of my childhood began about the age of six. Born in 1928, the height of the roaring twenties, a year before the stock market crash and onset of the Great Depression, my birth placed me at the dividing line of two American historical periods. I was the youngest in a family of three, with my older sister Hilma Marie and an older brother, Erling. My father Herman was a country doctor, with his specialty being a baby doctor—in his lifetime he delivered more than 600 babies into the world. My mother, Inga, a marvelous woman, was a school teacher. At the time of their marriage, my dad was 50 years old and my mother was 30, and when I came along my dad was 56 and my mother was 36. I was never told if my arrival in the world was planned or unplanned.

On the prairies of west central Minnesota, our family lived in Cyrus which had a population of about 350. The great majority of the inhabitants were Norwegian-Lutheran. As a youngster, it was commonplace to hear Norwegian spoken on the streets and in community gatherings. Both of my parents were fluent in Norwegian, and they spoke in Norwegian when they wanted to discuss things we children should not hear.

As I became an adult, I once asked my mother why we weren't taught Norwegian at home. She told me that she and my dad didn't want their children to grow up with an accent, as the big push was to Americanize youth and de-emphasize foreign cultures. I later discovered that these two ideas were prevailing myths in these days. It was ironic that neither of my parents had an accent. I regret not learning Norwegian.

My first twelve years of education took place in the Cyrus public school. Conveniently, we lived only two blocks from school. My first-grade teacher, Irene Mary Bjorgaard, was also my neighbor. Her mother, Mary Margaret, was my mother's best friend. Her father, Oscar Bjorgaard, was the president of Cyrus State Bank. Irene was a dark-haired petite woman with excellent teaching abilities, and everyone respected and loved her. One day Irene was wearing a pretty knit dress and standing in front of the blackboard with her back to the class. I approached her with a flat library book and whacked her backside. To me, it was a joke. Needless to say, Miss Bjorgaard was not amused. She became angry, turned around, and gave me a good shaking. I learned my lesson and that behavior was never repeated.

My third and fourth grade teacher, Miss Edith Swanson, was a rather tall, attractive sturdy boned woman. She projected a motherly image and had a pleasant, warm voice. It didn't take me long to develop a crush on her.

Two big events for a boy in Cyrus were getting guns (a BB gun and a 22 rifle) and learning to drive a car. I had a BB gun at about age 10 and had my own 22 rifle at age 12. The lessons of gun training and gun safety were delivered word-of-mouth, courtesy of village elders. Besides shooting at birds and rabbits, our favorite pasttime was going to the village dump to shoot bottles and tin cans. An abandoned 1930 Model T Ford was riddled with bullet holes. We called it John

Dillinger's car. We were fortunate that none of the bullets ricocheted back at us or any of the spectators.

I earned my first drivers' license in 1942 at the age of 14 for a fee of 35 cents. There was no driver's test or written examination required. When I was just twelve years old, my friend Freddie Tinseth, a local farmer, taught me how to drive by permitting me to drive his antique Ford pickup truck in the grain fields at threshing time. Once I held my driver's license, I became the official family chauffeur taking my dad on house calls and driving everyone on our family vacations.

The summer of the 1930s were hot and dry. While Cyrus did not have a swimming pool, young boys were not to be denied a place to swim. In the small Chippewa River, on the east side of Cyrus, rested a swimming hole of long-standing that had been enjoyed by hundreds of boys and sometimes girls for many summers. The swimming hole was about 60 feet across with a depth of seven feet. With a heavy rainfall the river would became swollen and rise a couple of feet. The large branch of a boxelder tree jutted out about five feet above the water. A favorite sport was to crawl out on the branch and jump into the water. As long as it was always boys, no bathing suits were even worn.

As I view my boyhood days, it was quite a sight to see nearly twenty boys in the nude sitting on the river bank and swimming. While I never asked permission of my mother to go swimming, late in the afternoon she would take one look at my hair and say "Llewellyn, you have been swimming at the Chippewa, haven't you." Even when I pled guilty, my mother handed down no sanctions.

One swimming hole incident that stands out in my memory occurred on a day in April. Despite air temperatures in the seventies, ice floes and chunks floated down the river. On that day some of us took off our clothes to go for a swim. My buddy, Abner, alias Yocum, got brave and managed to stand on a floating piece of ice in the altogether and calmly floated a good distance. It was the oddity of oddities to see a naked boy on a chunk of ice floating down the river.

On another occasion, in our grade school days, a group of us bought a plug of chewing tobacco for a dime. We then went down by the Chippewa River to try our chewing tobacco. Yocum was the first boy to bite of a piece of plug. We all took a chew. After chewing it for a little while, I can still see Yocum bent over vomiting and handing it behind his back to me. His face was a light shade of green. I took the plug, took another bite, and passed it on to my friends. It was not a pleasant experience for any of us.

In the 1930s and 40s, the local farmers harvested their grain by cutting and putting it into bundles and shocks, which were then put through a grain-threshing machine. Mountainous straw stacks dotted the countryside at this time of year. One day Yocum in his happy-go-lucky mode took his dad's shiny and mint condition Model A for a drive in the country and he got diverted into a field and began to drive around a straw stack. Unfortunately, the car got stuck in the pile. Yocum went for help, but when he returned the straw stack was in complete flames. The loss of the stack was negligible, but the car was a total loss. I never heard how Yocum's parents handled the situation.

Cyrus did not have a formal youth recreational center. Outdoors, we played the usual pick-up yard games, and in the winter we went ice-skating and snow-sliding. For indoor recreation, as boys would have it, they congregated at the local pool hall operated by Arnold "Inky" Ettesvold. He was called Inky because of his dark black hair. There were two pool tables that were seldom unused. It was a 3.2 beer joint where soft drinks and hot dogs were also sold. There was no minimum age limit to play pool and it was fun to play eight ball, smear, and other pool games. It was the gathering spot for farmers, business people, hired hands, and other town people. In this essentially "men and boys only" environment I learned the basis of American profanity. I heard every profane word one can imagine except the F word, which had not come into vogue. All of us teenagers became junior pool sharks. Richard Nixon once used the adverse expression of "pool hall language". That was a fortunate part of my early training in the male culture of rural America.

With America's de facto entry into World War II on December 7, 1941, life in Cyrus changed dramatically. The saddest part of that era was having the town's young men go off to war with twelve of them making the ultimate sacrifice. Essentials of life, including coffee, sugar, butter, meat, gasoline, tires and shoes, were in short supply so they had to be rationed. However, because Cyrus was located in a farming community, there was never a shortage of meat or butter.

As a young boy, I made my spending money by mowing lawns, shoveling snow, and cleaning out Avok's chicken coop every summer. In the summers of 1942 and 1943 my Uncle John Kjera called upon me to help harvest grain. When I was fourteen, with my cousins, Carolyn and Muriel Kjera, we spent long days placing grain bundles upright—8 to 10 bundles to a shock. Then in August, we performed the grain threshing. My boyhood friend Burdell Skogstad and I were assigned a team of horses with a hay rack to pick up bundles in the field and unload them into a threshing machine. The season lasted two to three weeks from farm to farm. At each farm every meal time, the tables were laden with all kinds of delicious food. My Aunt Sophie was an outstanding cook, and every worker looked forward to her banquet-style meals.

In the summers of 1944 and 1945 I was employed as an assistant butter maker at the Cyrus creamery which was owned and operated by Gib Ahlstrand. We worked long days on a six-day work week, closing only on Sundays. Two days a week I drove a truck to the country side to buy cream and eggs. Although I didn't have the opportunity for any farmer's daughter experiences, it did give me a chance to meet a variety of farm families. In the fall Gib and I would go out to farms at night to buy chickens. To load chickens we had to wait until it was dark when the chickens were roosted. Picking chickens off their roosts and loading them into crates produced a lot of dust and noise.

During these years I had a small paper route delivering the Minneapolis Tribune. Every Sunday morning the papers were left at Schwalbe's Café. Because of the war, most of the café's employees were high school boys and girls, who opened up the restaurant. Before beginning my route, my friends would give me a complimentary glass of 3.2 beer. Two things happened—I acquired some basic business experience and an introduction to beer.

I learned to dance the foxtrot at Schwalbe's Café. My classmate and special friend Wanda Alfson, who served as a waitress and cook of light lunches, taught me the steps. When business was slack, we would put a nickel in the juke box and dance to the music on the linoleum floor of the kitchen. Our favorite songs were "Blue Skies" and "Stardust". Everytime I hear these pieces I fondly remember my youthful days of dancing with Wanda. Wanda was an impressive young woman who had it all—good looks, personality, intelligence, and musical talent. Learning to dance was a necessary prerequisite to my attending dances at the Lakeside Ballroom in Glenwood, because many of the young men were off to war, and there were about four women to every man at the dances. At the time, I didn't realize what a golden opportunity it was to have a wide choice of dance partners.

The war created a teacher shortage, particularly in small school systems. However, we were fortunate in Cyrus to have Lillian Landahl as our high school principal, who had been a Lutheran missionary in China before being forced back to the states by the Japanese War Machine. She was a sister of Marion Haaland, the wife of Rev. Haaland, and was biding her time in Cyrus until the war was over. My high school had about 50 students in grades nine to twelve. Our class of 1946 had twelve students. The girls were: Wanda Alfson, Helen Olson, Helen Anderson, Clarice Hanson, Selma Amerson, Gloria Larson, Gen Skogstad, and Dorothy Johnson. The boys were: Allan Berg, Jerome Kjeldahl and Duane Solvie, and myself. Clarice Hanson was the valedictorian and Allan Berg was the salutatorian. We were a close-knit group not only because we had all of our classes together, but because we were all Norwegian Lutherans. I would liken our group to one of brothers and sisters. One of the best teachers of my entire academic career was my fifth and sixth grade teacher Kathryn Kaltenhauser. She had the exceptional ability to motivate students to acquire vast amounts of information and knowledge. Later she married Gib Ahlstrand, owner of the local creamery.

In spite of the war and the various shortages, boys' high school sports—football, basketball, and baseball—were played with much energy and enthusiasm, even if our win-loss records weren't always the best. Because there weren't many boys in our high school everyone had the chance to play in every sport. Unfortunately, at the time, high school girls were denied the opportunity to participate in sports. Cyrus in those years had a six man football team—every player was an eligible receiver with a three man line and a three man backfield. I played center compared to the traditional eleven-man games, and there was high scoring. In the fall of 1944, Allan Berg and I made a pact that we would not shave our mainly peach fuzz beards until we won a football game. It was good thing that we finally later that fall we finally decided to shave, because we lost 13 straight games during the 1944 and 1945 seasons. Our coach didn't know much about the game and neglected to put our team in adequate physical condition. After every game I was sore and ached all over—like I had been in a heavy street brawl.

We did better in basketball. At 6 feet, Allan Berg was our tallest player. Wayne "Pete" Bright was our star player and set some local scoring records. In our final year of 1945–46 we played 21 games, and our five losses were only by one point. Whether it was a lack of funds or poor administration, we did not have baseball uniforms, instead having to play our games in jeans. "Pete" Bright pitched many of the games, and I recall we had a .500 record.

Coming from a musical family, I experienced early and intense exposure to all sorts of music, but mainly classical. My dad played violin and gave music lessons. At about age 10, it was decided that I should take up the violin; but after one lesson it was determined that I wasn't suited to becoming a violin player. My mother played the piano and was our church organist for many years. My brother, Erling, a flutist, and my sister, Hilma, a vocalist and piano player, went on to become professional musicians and music teachers. Not to be neglected, I began to take piano lessons as a first grader from Eva Folin Pederson. Early on, it was determined that I was not all that musically endowed, but Eva exercised much patience with me week after week. Eva, truly a woman of God, assigned a wide variety of hymns from the Lutheran Concordia Hymnal for me to play. Since then, when I attended church on Sunday mornings, I often hear hymns that I learned from Eva. Almost all of us sang in the church choir, my friends included. From high school, I have fond memories of singing in a quartet with Allan Berg, Wanda Alfson and Helen Olson.

Going to Sunday school before church services as a young boy brings back pleasant memories. My mother was the Sunday School Superintendent during many of those years. She was highly respected and loved. Beginning in the eighth grade and continuing through the ninth grade, my schoolmates and I took confirmation lessons from Rev. Haaland for two hours every Saturday. Our main text was Luther's Small Catechism, which we had to memorize word for word. The whole objective of these lessons was to gain sufficient knowledge and understanding of our faith so as to be able to confirm the baptism vows made by our godparents and parents when we were just infants. Rev. Haaland, at six-foot four, was a rather physically imposing man who seldom smiled and always spoke rather seriously. In retrospect, he had a deep love for us and wanted to put us on the right track in life. In the spring of 1943, before the rite of confirmation was held, our class was publicly examined in front of the whole congregation on five consecutive Friday evenings. We had to recite Luther's Small Catechism by memory. Our class experienced high anxiety at these times, but we all survived.

U.S. Army Air Corps

I count myself very fortunate that I was too young to go off to military service in World War II. In November 1941, my brother Erling enlisted for six years in the Navy. Because of his talent as a flute player and his training at the Navy School of Music in Washington, D.C., he spent most of WWII in a Navy band at Recife, Brazil.

Since I turned age 18 on May 11, 1946 and the draft law was due to expire May 15, 1946, it was certain that I would be drafted into the Army that summer or fall. At that time, the U.S. Army Air Corps (in 1947 it became the U.S. Air Force) was running full page newspaper ads offering that with a three year enlistment, a person would receive 48 months of the educational G.I. Bill and the right to choose a training school. Because my dad kept informal weather records for years, I wanted to become a weather observer. The idea of 48 months of free college was a big incentive since our family had limited financial resources. The offer was almost too good to be true. So a few days after I finished high school, I boarded a bus for Fort Snelling to join the Air Force. On June 6, I was sworn into the service with the serial number of 17172676.

During my first days at Fort Snelling, I was given a physical examination, written tests, and my uniforms. I remember well standing in line, with just a bath towel wrapped around my middle, to receive vaccinations in each of my arms. A tall, skinny recruit standing a few feet in front of me passed out when he got a close look at the medics administering the shots. The hearing test was different. It took place in a room about 10 by 25 feet. I was asked to stand in the corner facing the outside wall. The medic stood at the other end of the room. The test consisted of his whispering numbers—like 03, 31, 48—and then asking me to report them. Then the test was repeated by my standing in the other corner, thereby exposing the other ear. Right in front of me, at each station, was an adult sized poster of an attractive, frontally nude woman. I passed the hearing test, but I am still wondering whether the test was medically accurate.

Then it was off to Kelly AFB, San Antoinio, Texas for six weeks of basic training. Every Friday night we had a G.I. party in our barracks, which meant scrubbing the floors and washing the windows. Most of the men in my flight of 65 were from the South. Our typical day was filled with military classes and a lot of drilling–left-right-about face-attention-at ease-all the familiar terms of training. The summer of 1946 in Texas was extremely hot, and we had rain only once. It was the first and only time I ever broke out with a heat rash on my stomach, arms and legs. There were no long hikes or physical fitness classes. Since the war was over, six weeks of basic training was quite relaxed. I thought of it as a glorified Boy Scout camp.

Upon completion of basic training, I was transferred to Chanute Field, Illinois for weather observer's training. It was twelve-week course that taught us everything we needed to know about watching and noting the weather. We started out with 155 students, but only 36 completed the course. Some of the students did not apply themselves and others discovered that work in a weather station was not their calling. Like a ritual, every Friday morning we were given a comprehensive test of the past weeks' classes. If a student failed the test, that person was dropped from the class. There were no second chances.

Upon graduation from weather observer's school in late fall of 1946, I was transferred to Tinker AFB, Oklahoma City for assignment to a weather station. In mid-January 1947, eight of us were transferred to Westover AFB, Springfield, Massachusetts for an actual assignment. Captian Beneke, the officer-in-charge, who acted more like a friendly high school principal than a military man, had the job of making our assignments. In his office at the onset, he flatly stated that five of us were going to weather outposts in Northern Canada and Greenland, and three of us were going to Presque Isle AFB, Presque Isle, Maine.

Surprisingly everyone wanted go to either Northern Canada or Greenland. Nobody wanted the Maine assignment. After 30 minutes of compromise, Capt. Beneke said that we should settle it by pulling the names out of a hat. You guessed it— I pulled out Presque Isle. In retrospect it was hard to believe why anyone would want to be stationed in a far northern weather station where, in the winter, food, other supplies, and mail had to be dropped by airplane on a weekly basis. Presque Isle is in the northern tip of Maine, about 25 miles from the Canadian border. By latitude it was on the same level as Bemidji, Minnesota. During World War II it was a stopping off point for planes flying to Europe. Since the end of the war, the base had greatly diminished, and when I arrived it had only a complement of 125 men and all of us were quartered in a wood base hospital.

From a climate point of view, stationed in Presque Isle

was much like the hardy winters in Cyrus. There was always a lot of snow, and in the winter of 1948 we had a period of two weeks where the temperature never went above 0 degrees Fahrenheit. During that same time period, there was a week of night-time temperatures in the low minus 40s. In the summer the temperature never got above 90 degrees. There was very little military air traffic, and Northeast Airlines had an outgoing morning flight and an incoming flight. Weather reports were sent out on an hourly basis, and if there were any drastic weather changes, reports were sent out more frequently. Our call letters were DZQ, and we were on the same teletype sequence with such airports as Logan Field, Boston and La Guardia, New York City. It was big stuff for a country boy from Cyrus. Since we were basically a small operation, there were never more than six weather observers and two weather forecasters. In my duties, I made surface weather observations and prepared weather charts which the forecasters used to make their predictions. In 1947 we started to calculate the windchill temperatures, which is now used universally.

Social life in Presque Isle, estimated population of 3000, was rather limited. The enlisted men's club in base was one of our main social centers. My friend, Elton Gissendanner from Georgia, and I made friends with twin women, Glenda and Glenna from Caribou, Maine located twelve miles north of Presque Isle. (Sorry I can't remember their last name). I dated Glenda, a petite, pretty red head. We did a lot of dancing, and she taught me how to jitter bug. Her family was very kind to us and entertained us on a regular basis. I also became acquainted with members of a Swedish-American family, whom I met while attending a Lutheran church. I enjoyed many delicious meals and pleasant outings with this family.

By the summer of 1948 I was promoted to Sergeant, and

all of a sudden, in July I received orders for transfer to Chanute AFB in Illinois to be an instructor at the weather observer's school. I never did get a satisfactory explanation why I was transferred. However, I appreciated the move because it brought me closer to Minnesota and removed me from those dreaded graveyard shifts. At Chanute I was given a charge of five instructors and a class of 50 students. I was also promoted to Staff Sergeant. As a joke we referred to ourselves as professors, and I took the title of Professor of Surface Observations. To my later amazement, I could give a one hour lecture on how to report the different types of drizzle.

An additional pleasant advantage in the transfer to Chanute was that my dad's only sister, Aunt Martha Linde Frazee, lived only 120 miles away in Indianapolis, Indiana. Nearby also lived many of my cousins and their families. I spent almost every weekend in Indianapolis with relatives. My main mode of transportation was hitch-hiking, and with my Air Force Uniform, cars seldom passed me by. The cousins I visited most were Bob Frazee and his wife Dorothea Ann, and Glenn Frazee and his wife Helen. My cousins were very hospitable and always showed me a good time.

In the spring of 1949 my thoughts turned to the end of my three year enlistment and setting up my future education plans. I was fortunate to have 48 months of free education in my hip pocket. So that spring I applied for admission to Concordia College, Moorhead and was accepted. Since my brother Erling was a second year student there, and my dad finished Concordia in 1898, the decision was not difficult.

On May 14, 1949 I was honorably discharged at Chanute AFB at the rank of Staff Sergeant and was given $279 in severance pay. I then took a sentimental trip back to northern Maine to visit old friends and see old familiar sights. From there I crossed into Canada through the cities of Quebec City and Montreal. I continued into northern Michigan to Duluth. From there I traveled to Minneapolis and then home to Cyrus. The Canadian trip was wonderful, and I enjoyed the people and locales. It was good to be back home again. I got my old job back at the creamery and settled in for the summer, eagerly awaiting my Concordia College education.

THE PURSUIT OF
HIGHER EDUCATION

In the fall of 1949, I enrolled at Concordia College in Moorhead. One of the very positive things about going to college was that all of my expenses of tuition, books, board and room were covered by the G.I. Bill. It also was a good feeling to know that I had completed my military obligation—luckily during peace time.

Since my brother Erling had just finished his second year at Concordia, I enjoyed the advantage of moving into the same rooming house and making his friends my friends. Our landlady "Ma" Anna Redman was a warm and kind lady, but ran things with a velvet iron fist. While most of the roomers were veterans, we were of legal drinking age. She did not allow any beer or liquor on the premises, but she understood if some of us came back to the house after a night of celebrating, she could have just as easily turned us in to Dean Victor Boe. Most of us followed the principle of "study first, play second."

Our first year class had 333 students, and our final graduating class was 150 students. On the first day in an assembly, we were told that 75% of our group were either salutatorians or valedictorians. I never told anyone that I finished seventh in a class of twelve at Cyrus High School. One of the rewards of Concordia was the chance to meet some remarkable men and women, many of whom became lifetime friends.

When I started college I did not have any definite idea of what professional career I wanted to pursue, but I was leaning towards pre-law. As time went on, my major became history and political science with a minor in speech. I had accumulated enough psychology and education credits to enable me to secure a license to teach social studies and speech.

My studies were interrupted by war. At the end of the first semester of my sophomore year, at the height of the Korean War, I took an extended leave from college to work as a weather observer for the U.S. Weather Bureau at Wake Island. A refueling stop for planes crossing the Pacific Ocean, Wake Island was only ten square miles in area and was located approximately 2000 miles west of the Hawaiian Islands. Wake Island's highest point was a mere ten feet above sea level. While I made excellent wages, two hours after I was on the island, I regretted leaving my studies. I never got accustomed to the tropical climate, and I always perspired—even while wearing just a t-shirt and shorts. I had signed an agreement to stay for one year. In September of 1951 my mother developed some serious health problems, and I returned to Concordia.

One could write a long chapter on each of my different classes and professors, stories sometimes humorous and at other times sad. The most important feature of Concordia was that every class was small, where it was easy to get to know a teacher on a first name basis. No question about it, the professors were underpaid, but dedicated to their calling. All of the professors were highly motivated to help each student achieve his or her highest potential. By and large, they were wonderful role models. The following professors made the greatest impression on me:

Harding Noblitt A PhD graduate from the University of Chicago, who was always full of political jokes. His best was about Benito Mussolini: "I can't tell you in what part of his body he got wounded in World War I, but I can tell you how it happened."

Marie Braaten My French teacher, who was born and raised in Madagascar, and her parents were Lutheran missionaries. Still in her 20s, she was a looker. She spoke beautiful French, but not much rubbed off on me.

Thomas Burgess A psychology professor who also was professional hypnotist. He had the belief that a clinical psychologist was the end-all of the mental health field and he downed psychiatrists on a regular basis. In spite of some of his misguided ideas, he taught me a lot about human behavior.

Raidar Thomte A philosophy professor of the first rank who was a leading authority on the Danish Theologian Soren Kierkegaard. He had a great sense of humor and once described Christian Science thought as "what is matter never mind, and what is mind never matter." In the summer of 1952, we made political bets on the Presidential campaign with cigars which we both enjoyed.

Professor Fugelstad A very proud and learned biology professor, who always bragged about the number of biology students who went on to become medical doctors. As a senior, in my final semester of biology, I was doing failing work. I had no interest in the course. I went to him expressing my fear that a failing grade would prevent my graduation from college. His understanding response was, "Don't worry, you will get a passing grade." What a wonderful gift.

One experience which stands out in my memory was the day that about 20 of us were in Professor Dordahl's class for our three week teaching assignments. As he called off the names and locations, some of us let out muffled groans when we weren't given our first choices. One by one each of my classmates left the room after receiving their posting. When it came to the point when I was the only one left in the room, he asked me, "Lew, do you still want to go to Cyrus?" With no hesitation, I said yes. It meant that I could go to my home high school and stay at home. It happened that Professor Dordahl was a good friend of Allen Graves, the Cyrus Superintendent of Schools. The practice teaching took place in January 1953 and on a beautiful day, June 1, 1953, I graduated from Concordia College with a Bachelor of Arts Degree.

On To Law School

In 1919 my mother worked in Washington, D.C. as a clerk in the war department. This was before she returned to Cyrus to care for her mother, Anne, before she married my dad in 1922. While in the nation's capitol she took night classes in English Literature at George Washington University. She always recounted this experience with pleasure. My plans to attend George Washington University Night Law School were largely inspired by her comments. Borrowing her enthusiasm, I applied and was accepted by GWU Night Law School. It was my intention to secure a daytime government job and attend law school in the evenings.

In August 1953 I traveled to Washington to try to secure a job in preparation for night school. At that time, President Eisenhower had laid off 8000 government employees, and it was impossible to beg, borrow or steal a job. I spent ten days pounding the pavement looking for work. My Cyrus friend, Sam Ronnie, lived in Virginia, and he offered to let me live with him and his family until I got a job even if it became indefinite. In spite of his kind offer, I couldn't stand the uncertainty. I then returned to St. Paul where I immediately found employment with State Farm Insurance Company as an office underwriter. At the same time I was admitted to the St. Paul College of Law under the G.I. Bill.

The St. Paul College of Law was located in an old mansion near downtown St. Paul next to Miller Hospital. I managed to rent a room a block away from the law school. Classes were held Mondays through Fridays from 7:00 P.M. to 9:00 P.M. Most of the professors came from law firms, and some were sitting judges. Most of them mainly followed the socratic method of teaching, without defining the idea. Needless to say, if a student wasn't prepared to recite in class, what followed was a round of sarcasm, intimidation, and humiliation delivered by the professor to the poor student. Because of this merciless approach, our class had dwindled from 72 to 36 students by Thanksgiving break. I spent most weekends and evenings that year trying to stay ahead of those tough professors.

I made it through the first year with respectable grades. I must give thanks to my fellow classmate, Bill Von Arx, a very bright man, who gave me some excellent mentoring. Bill became a lifelong friend and was the best man at my wedding. My first job at State Farm wasn't what I had anticipated. After the first Christmas, my supervisor, a nice enough

man, took me aside and said even though my job performance was acceptable, he could sense that I would be better
suited to another field. He told me that I could take time off
from the job to look for employment. While at Concordia, I
took a Social Worker examination and was qualified to work
in any of Minnesota County Welfare Departments. I went to
Ramsey County Welfare Department in St. Paul and was offered a job. On February 1, 1954, I became a public assistance caseworker.

Without realizing it at the time, the new job was the beginning of a lifetime career spent dealing with a variety of
people and their social problems. On the first day of work my
supervisor, Tonette Hall, a pleasant lady, gave me a choice of
beginning to read policy manuals or making my first home
visit. I selected the home visit, which consisted of seeing an
elderly grandfather and his sixteen-year-old unmarried pregnant granddaughter in a run-down apartment. There was no
evidence that this was an incest situation. Needless to say, it
was a nerve racking experience. The vast majority of my caseload consisted of nearly 350 old-age assistance cases. I had to
provide a financial review of each case on an annual basis.

My designated area was in the St. Paul Cathedral district
which contained a number of small apartment complexes.
Most of my clients were women, but I had one unforgettable
Irish man, who spoke with brogue. He made a few extra dollars by making and selling Plaster-of-Paris wall plaques.
My favorite one inscribed the inscription "God Bless Our
Mortgaged Home." I also followed a limited number of cases
from the Aid to Families With Dependent Children, Aid to
the Blind, Aid to the Disabled and General Relief programs.
The basis of my involvement in these cases was to determine
their present and continued eligibility to receive financial

assistance. Evident in many of the situations was a variety of social problems that plagued their lives.

Working at the Ramsey County Welfare Department gave me the chance to work with some interesting colleagues. It was my first opportunity to work with people from other races and cultures. Three well-remembered and remarkable persons were Pearl Mitchell and John Patton, African-Americans, and Elvira Mercado, a Hispanic. Being with these people every day taught me much about their cultures. In connection with my work, I formed a delightful relationship with Mary M. Ashford, a medical social worker at Ancker Hospital. We enjoyed many good times together.

In the spring of 1955, I read an informational bulletin from the State of Minnesota, which was offering two-year scholarships to obtain a Masters Degree in social work. The specific purpose was to recruit psychiatric social workers for Minnesota State Mental Hospitals. At this juncture in my life, I was discovering a strong pull towards social work and the idea of becoming a lawyer was no longer appealing. A scholarship to cover all of my educational and living expenses was a strong incentive. I applied for the program and was accepted. That June I completed two years at the St. Paul College of Law and was awarded a Bachelors of Science in Law Degree. This is the preliminary degree before earning the Juris Doctor degree upon finishing law school. At the same time I was admitted to the Indiana University School of Social Work at Indianapolis. I chose IU because my Aunt Martha and many cousins lived in Indianapolis. My parents and close friends thought it was a great idea.

In the fall of 1955, I went to Indianapolis to enter graduate school. While the main IU campus was located in Bloomington, Indiana, the school of social work was in an office building in downtown Indianapolis. Seeing as how the school was off-campus, it was similar to attending a business college in a downtown area. Only at final exam time when our answer books said IU did I realize that I was part of a much larger university.

Soon after starting classes, I was pleased with my new educational plan. My class size was 25 students, the majority being women and I being one of only six men. One fourth of the class was African American. We were a very compatible group united in our dedication to alleviate the suffering of society's disadvantaged and poor. We used to call our school a branch of the University of Chicago School of Social Work. From Dean Mary Houk all the way down the line, most of the faculty members were University of Chicago graduates. The graduate school policy followed Chicago's philosophy with its emphasis in students becoming professionally skilled in counseling techniques rather than high academic achievement. A letter grade of C was acceptable, and there were very few As granted.

Still followed today in graduate schools of social work is the plan of three days per week in a field placement and the other two days in the classroom. Along with five other students, my first year placement was in the Marian County (Indianapolis) Juvenile Court where I had a limited caseload of juvenile boys. My field worker, Merritt Gilman, also became my father-confessor and personal coach, and he was a wonderful man. An old saying goes that in social work training they take a student's ego apart and put it back together before graduation. I learned to deeply admire Merritt Gilman for his kindness and understanding. At the court I became friends with Eunice Hoise, a probation officer. Eunice will always hold a special place in my Indiana memories, because of a close personal relationship and the nice times together.

As students, we sat in a large conference room with telephones where we wrote our process records, held student conferences and received telephone calls. One morning when all of my fellow students were present, there was a note at my place to contact a Miss Rose. I thought it was a call from a parent, teacher or police officer about a case of mine. I called the listed number and asked if I could speak with Miss Rose. The voice at the other rend said that she wasn't presently available. At that point, my fellow students were all looking at me with big grins, and they began to laugh. They had given me the telephone number of the Fox Burlesque Theatre where Rose LaRose was the headline stripper.

In a variety of courses, we learned such topics as casework (counseling), social research, social work history and policy, group work, and psychiatry. In my first semester, one of our instructors was a psychiatrist, Dr. David Phillips, who taught human behavior. The course was unique because we were taught the basis of Sigmund Freud's theories. We were explicitly instructed to use Freudian theories in dealing with our clients. We learned all of the fundamental principles behind, oral, anal, eclectic, id, ego, and super ego ideas. Shortly after my graduation in 1957, the Freudian concepts became obsolete. To this day I still like the idea that the ego is the battleground in a person's mind between the primal urges of the id and the restraints of the super ego.

During my Indiana days I became friends with two special people. Wayne Johnson, from Sioux City, Iowa and Bonnie Becker Cacavas from Aberdeen, South Dakota. Wayne, a year ahead of me, and I shared an apartment in my second year. Wayne was a probation officer in the Marian County Juvenile Court and later became a professor of social work at the University of Iowa. I also had the privilege of being

Wayne's best man at his marriage to his lovely wife Donna in 1959. Bonnie had a friendly and warm personality, and was elected May Day Queen in college. Our Midwest connection strongly influenced our friendship. We used to travel back and forth from Indianapolis to our hometowns at holiday times. At the first Thanksgiving, the Milwaukee Railroad was running a special ticket price of one ticket full-fare with the second ticket being half-fare for a married couple. At that time, both headed for St. Paul, we approached the ticket window at Indianapolis where I said, "I want to buy two round trip tickets for my wife and me to Minneapolis." Without any questions, the agent sold me two special-priced tickets.

I spent the summer of 1956 back in St. Paul working at my old job in the Ramsey County Welfare Department. Returning that fall to IU, I was assigned a field work placement in medical social work at the Indianapolis VA hospital.

Working in a medical setting was fascinating and I learned many new things about illness, especially ways in which disabilities affect individuals and their families. My fear of seeing blood, open sores and physical disabilities was fully exposed during this placement. I did find out that I could work effectively in situations where the suffering and disabilities were hidden. My field work instructor at the time, Margaret Neville, was nearing retirement age. She was a close personal friend of Charlotte Towle, a social work pioneer. While we never had a close teaching relationship, she gave me much freedom in dealing with patients. While painful at times, she did an admirable performance of putting my ego back together.

Graduate students often find that completion of a thesis becomes a stumbling block in obtaining a degree. Our class did a group thesis with the friendly help of our advisor, Genevieve Weeks. We evaluated 300 referrals of children from kindergarten to third grade to the Indianapolis Public School Social Service Department for the school year of 1955-1956. They presented a wide range of social problems. The idea was that, if possible, these students would be followed until they completed high school. We also sat for a full day of written comprehensive examinations in addition to an hour of oral comprehensive examinations, just before graduation.

My graduation with a Master of Arts degree took place on June 10, 1957 at Bloomington. Joyfully, my mother came to Indiana for graduation. Wayne Johnson took me, my mother and Aunt Martha to Bloomington. It was a beautiful day. Graduation was in the football stadium in an outdoor ceremony. On our way back to Indianapolis we stopped in Martinsville for a delicious chicken dinner.

My Indiana experience was pleasant and left me with many cherished memories.

Meeting

Marcella

MEETING MARCELLA

With my MSW in hand, my return to Minnesota in June 1957 meant no more academics, but now full employment. To fulfill the terms of my scholarship I had to spend two years as a psychiatric social worker in a state mental hospital. I could begin working in any one of the state hospitals such as St. Peter, Fergus Falls or Anoka. I selected the Hastings State Hospital mainly for one reason: it would permit me to resume my legal education at the William Mitchell College of Law (formerly the St. Paul College of Law). Initially, when I went to Indiana, I planned to give up the study of law, but my professors at IU strongly recommended that I finish my law degree. They believed that a person with social work and law degrees could be beneficial to society.

On July 1, 1957 I arrived at the Hastings State Hospital in my 1951 Chevrolet Coupe, with clothes, books, and $130.00 in my bank account. I appreciated a fringe benefit of the job; living in the employee quarters with board and room, plus laundry, which cost me only $31.00 per month. In the social service unit there were four professional social workers along with our supervisor Nate Mandel. Nate was a seasoned and well-trained professional who treated his staff exceptionally well. He also had a wonderful sense of humor and always started the day off with a couple of very funny jokes.

The dress code was a shirt and tie, dress slacks, and a white clinic coat. I was assigned to the geriatric unit, which housed approximately 350 patients out of a total 1000 in the whole hospital. Most of the patients, for whom I had professional responsibility, had been diagnosed with senile dementia and were housed in locked wards. My role was to gather a social history from the family of the patient, upon commitment, explain the role of the hospital, and most importantly, help the family deal with the guilt of committing their loved one.

When a patient was recommended for a conditional release to a nursing home, I helped make the placement plans. Most of my patients expired in the hospital. I was placed with Dr. Joseph Delougherty, Chief of the Geriatric Unit. The patients and staff loved him for his kindness and understanding. He was easy to work with and had a wonderful sense of humor.

In the 1940s and 1950s it was common for the State of Minnesota to hire physicians in their mental hospitals who were former recovered alcohol or drug addicts. Dr. Delougherty was unique because he was the only staff physician at Hastings without a past history of chemical abuse. Most of his professional career was spent in the Middle East, before his early retirement, where he was a doctor for an American oil company. He had an exceptional understanding of mental illness and its treatment.

Working and living at a mental hospital with nearly 1000 patients and several hundred staff members marked the beginning of a new career for me. The hospital staff was always looking for creative ways to keep our patients fully occupied while being treated full-time. For those patients well enough to leave the wards, they enjoyed plenty of free time to walk around the scenic wooded grounds. During the first week of my employment, I attended orientation classes and took tours of the hospital along with several other new employees. On a warm sunny day, while our guide was showing us a facility, a middle-aged male patient, nordic looking and neat appearing, dressed in his street clothes, walked by us noticing our newness. He took us all by surprise when he said in a loud and clear voice, "I'm not going to take any shit from anybody." It was the kind of verbal directive one would like to use at certain times, but one would think twice before saying it because of the negative consequences.

Once a week our medical director presided over morning staff meetings to review unique and challenging cases. He would present the person's history and interview the patient. Staff attendance was limited to doctors, psychologists, social workers, rehabilitation supervisors, and nursing supervisors. It was at one of those early staff meetings when I first noticed Marcella, a psychiatric nursing instructor. I have a clear remembrance of a beautiful woman in her white starched uniform and cap. She had natural wavy auburn hair, a fair complexion with attractive blue eyes and lovely brown freckles. She was a looker. We were introduced at that time, and within a few weeks, we happened to meet in the hospital canteen for coffee. It was then that I found out that she was a widow with three small children, and I told her that I was a bachelor going to night law school. After that we had coffee together a few times. And, of course, we saw each other at work almost every day.

By October, I had become more attracted to her. I finally worked up enough nerve to ask her out for dinner. We made that first official date for a Saturday night. That afternoon she went to a football game at the University of Minnesota with Ben and Rosie Sontag and their first cousin Jack Gores and his wife Phyllis. Later that afternoon we met in downtown St. Paul and had dinner at the Hotel Lowry Driftwood room. While she was attractive in her nurses uniform, she was stunning in civilian clothes. That was the formal beginning of our courtship, which included going together to movies, concerts, athletic events, and out dancing. Also, I became new-found friends of her young children, Ken, Kay and Rick. On our first date, I brought them each a new toy: a slinky. I came to find out later that all three of them were impressed by me when I gave all of them the hottest new toy of the times, a slinky, on our first date. Later, at a family dinner in Rosemount, I met her swell parents, Ferd and Marie Ruhr.

Beth Kane, nursing school classmate and close friend of Marcella, was living in Hastings with her husband Joe when Marcella came to Hastings from Chicago. Out of economic necessity and a desire to continue in the nursing profession, Marcella considered several job opportunities. The sisters of Regina Hospital were eager to have her in their employ, but it meant evening and weekend hours. At the time, Beth was a nursing supervisor at the Hastings State Hospital. She encouraged Marcella to go to St. Paul and take the nursing instructor examination for training psychiatric aides. Marcella was reluctant about taking the examination, but, with Beth's urging, she went ahead. Marcella passed the examination easily and immediately was offered the instructors job at Hastings. Among other things, the job appealed to her because it was a Monday through Friday daytime job, which, of course, she accepted.

Despite her level of education and reasonable earning capacity, Marcella being an unmarried woman with children, found that banks and lending agencies would refuse to qualify her for a home mortgage. The frustrating part of this situation was that men even those with no education and making less pay, were treated more leniently by the banks.

Working as Dr. Delougherty's social worker, I spent much of my time with him making rounds to see his patients and providing consultation on social problems. Needless to say, we dealt with a wide variety of people and their difficulties. One case that stands out in my memory was on a day when we were making rounds to see patients. When interviewing a patient with severe cognitive problems, he checked her recognition ability by asking her the question, "Who am I?" Mary (not her real name) remained silent. Dr. Delougherty named the following persons: "Am I the nurse, the doctor, or the janitor?" Still no word from Mary as the different occupations were named. We stood by waiting for a response. Finally, in a dead pan delivery, she said, "Oh you are the man who collects the income taxes." Since Dr. Delougherty regularly complained about paying high income taxes, we had a good laugh over that one.

I also recall the day that I was gathering a social history from the husband of a newly admitted voluntary patient. Earlier in the day at her initial examination, it was determined that she might be pregnant so she was referred to a consulting gynecologist. During my history gathering with the husband he casually informed me that his wife had been examined by a "geologist" that morning.

Every patient who we dealt with came from a sad past with great exposure to suffering. Olivia (not her real name) was a woman in her early twenties who was admitted to the hospital with a diagnosis of chronic schizophrenia. She came from a culturally deprived family. For example, in grade school her fellow students called her "Stinky" because of her poor hygiene. Olivia looked the part of a model or movie star--naturally attractive with her light brown hair, pale blue eyes, fair complexion, a cute turned-up nose, and a schoolgirl figure. Her illness prevented her from reaching a better potential. Her situation, like many of the others I came across on a daily basis, filled my heart with sorrow.

Dr. Delougherty had deep respect for the well being of all of his patients and a full recognition of their worth as human beings. I clearly remember one of his patients, a young woman in her 20s with a diagnosis of mental illness, mild mental retardation and epilepsy. Elizabeth (not her real name) was the daughter of a professional man and had three siblings who were professionals. At a young age she developed problems with many hospitalizations. In response to the family concerns of her care in a state mental hospital, Dr. Delougherty wrote the following letter:

> Dear Mr. and Mrs. Smith (not their real names):
>
> Thank you for your recent letter about the welfare of your daughter, Elizabeth. I can understand your concern that she receive the best possible care. We will do everything within our resources to provide her with quality services.
>
> Elizabeth has suffered much in her young lifetime. We know that she is under the watchful protection of the Almighty and close to God's mercy seat.
>
> Sincerely yours,
> Dr. Joseph T. Delougherty

While Marcella and I dated and saw each other on a regular basis that first year, it wasn't until the fall of 1958 that we became serious and committed to each other. During this period of time, I resumed my night law school studies on a part time basis. We developed mutual friends from the hospital staff and went to house parties, summer picnics, and social events.

I also became well acquainted with Ken, Kay and Rick and enjoyed many family activities with them.

In early 1959 we began to talk about wedding plans and selected August 8 as our wedding date with St. Boniface Church to be the place for the ceremony. Taking on a ready-made family made the marriage an even bigger step for me. My love for Marcella and the children and knowing her competence, friendliness and beauty made the whole process much easier as we took the major step together. Marcella's first wedding had been a large affair, and she preferred that we have a smaller, more intimate wedding. The culture of the day dictated that a widow's second marriage should be low key. In early summer we began to make wedding plans in earnest. First, we needed to select the matron-of-honor and a best man. Since my brother Erling was not a Catholic, he could not serve as my best man. In his place I selected by good friend and law school classmate, Bill Von Arx. At her first wedding Marcella had her sister Rosie Sontag as her matron-of-honor. Since Rosie was very pregnant with Tom, she declined the honor. In her place Marcella chose her Aunt Hildegard Tierney, sister to Marie Ruhr. The next major task was generating the guest list. Since we were limited to 125 guests that could be accommodated at Eddie's Café, we found that narrowing down the guest list was difficult. We regretted that we could not invite more family and friends.

We met twice with Father Robert Blumeyer about the wedding ceremony. Since I was not a Catholic, the wedding rite would not include a Catholic mass. As a part of marrying Marcella, I had to sign an agreement that I would raise our children in the Catholic faith. I gladly consented to the promise. The easiest part of wedding plans was the music arrangements. My brother Erling played several music selections including

Norwegian folk tunes and his flute before the ceremony, and my sister Hilma sang two solos during the ceremony.

Just three months earlier, on May 10, 1959 my father died unexpectedly after a short illness. His absence was deeply felt. About six weeks before his death, Marcella, the children and I went to Cyrus where we enjoyed a pleasant visit with him and my mother.

The account of the wedding from the August 13, 1959 issue of the Hastings Gazette gives a nice description of that memorable day.

Linde-Schulzensohn Vows Exchanged
At St. Boniface Church

Marcella Ruhr Schulzensohn of Hastings, dauther of Mr. and Mrs. F. A. Ruhr of Rosemount, became the bride of Llewellyn H. Linde, son of Mrs. Herman Linde and the late Dr. Linde of Cyrus, Minnesota on Saturday, August 8th at St. Boniface Church, Hasitngs.

Rev. Robert Blumeyer, O.S.B. officiated at the double ring ceremony.

The bride, given in marriage by her father, wore a sapphire blue suit with matching accessories and a white orchid corsage. Her matron of honor was her aunt, Mrs. Gordon Tierney of Hastings, who was attired in a beige suite with matching accessories and a corsage of roses.

William V. Von Arx of St. Paul Park served as best man. Ushers were Joseph Ruhr of Los Angeles, brother of the bride and Benjamin Sontag of Hastings, brother-in-law of the bride. The men wore dark suits with white carnation boutonnieres.

The bride's mother wore a royal blue dress and the mother of the groom was attired in navy blue, both wore corsages of roses.

Erling H. Linde of Moorhead, brother of the groom, played several flute selections before the ceremony. Mrs. Russell K. Griswold of Brainerd, sister of the groom, sang Shubert's "Ave Maria" and Caesar's "Panis Angelicus." The organist was Mark Tominac of Hastings.

Following the ceremony, a reception was held in the Sierra Room, Eddie's Café.

The bride is a graduate of the College of St. Catherine and the St. Joseph's Hospital School of Nursing. The groom is a graduate of Concordia College, Moorhead and Indiana University School of Social Work. Both are on the staff at the Hastings State Hospital.

Following a wedding trip to northern Minnesota and Canada, the couple will be at home at 1610 Tyler Street, Hastings.

Lew and Marcella's wedding, August 8, 1959.

A New Family Arrangement

The transition from being a bachelor to joining a new family was made easy by joining the Ruhr family. I found Marcella's parents, Ferd and Marie Ruhr, to be very caring and positive. At the time of our marriage they lived in Rosemount, where Ferd was a retired banker with a long history of community service. In 1961 the Ruhrs moved to Hastings to be closer to our family and the Sontag family. Plus, Marie had her roots in Hastings, and Ferd was born and raised on a farm near Miesville, just a few miles out of town from Hastings. Marcella and Marie introduced me to the card game of Bridge. Marcella and I spent many Sunday afternoons playing Bridge with her parents. Marcella and Marie were particularly good players. Marie possessed the uncanny mental ability, after the first round of bidding, to almost tell precisely which player held the high cards. As one of her card-playing friends said at Marie's 1983 visitation prior to her funeral "Marie always held good cards."

The Ruhr, Sontag, and Linde families were closely knit. Christmas, Easter, and other special celebrations rotated between the three family homes. Since the three Linde children and the Sontag children were close in age, it made for available playmates at these festive occasions. In the early 1960s, Ben and Rosie Sontag purchased a summer lake home two hours away from Hastings near Amery, Wisconsin. Many pleasant family affairs were conducted at this location.

Although infrequent, trips to the Linde side of the family were made when possible. Because Mother Linde lived in Moorhead for many years, distance ruled against frequent contact. The Griswolds (Hilma and Russ and their three sons) lived at St. Croix Falls, Wisconsin. We visited back and forth more frequently and usually spent Thanksgiving together. Erling and Janice Linde lived in Moorhead, and the few visits there were always pleasurable. Mother Linde came from a family of 12 children. Her father Iver Hippe homesteaded a farm near Starbuck in central Minnesota in 1871, and later married his wife Anne. On a Sunday in June 1971 a Hippe Family Centennial was held at St. John's Lutheran Church near Starbuck. The weather was perfect—warm, but not hot—with a clear blue sky. A church service was held in the morning and a catered dinner was served at noon. A formal program was held in the afternoon, leaving plenty of time afterward for visiting. The five surviving children of Iver and Anne were present, along with 175 other descendants to make for a thrilling afternoon.

Fulfilling an important goal shortly after our wedding—of making all of us a family together in the eyes of the law—we began proceedings for me to legally adopt Ken, Kay and Rick. We engaged my law-school classmate, and our best man, Bill Van Arx to serve as our attorney. In mid-October, at a hearing before Judge Hiniker at the Dakota County Courthouse, the adoption became legal and final. Afterward, Bill and our legally-joined family dined together at a celebration lunch at the then Gardner Hotel. Although Marcella was completely in favor of the adoption, she found it difficult to accept the fact that the newly issued birth certificates eliminated the children's last name of Schulzensohn. We did retain their former birth certificates to note the historical change.

Lew's Working Years

WORKING YEARS AFTER 1959

After our marriage in 1959, both Marcella and I were employed at the State Hospital. We were fortunate to have the child care services of Lorena Willlison. She had a nice way with children and spent hours with them doing craft projects. Because of the distance between our home and the hospital, travel to and from work was easy.

I can't tell you exactly why, but a few months after our marriage, I took a position with the Minnesota Department of Public Welfare (DPW) in St. Paul as a consultant in their section on mental retardation. It was also my last year of night law school, and I spent three evenings each week going to classes. My consultation duties consisted mainly of dealing with county welfare departments on their guardianship cases. In those days, hundreds of mentally retarded patients resided in state hospitals in Faribault, Cambridge and Owatonna. About 50 children with Downs Syndrome age four to seven lived in a cottage near the Woman's Prison in Shakopee and were cared for by inmates. On those days when I made official trips to many of the state facilities, I was impressed by the high level of individual care provided to patients. Personally, I found it depressing to see hundreds of retarded individuals in one location. Nowadays, the mega institutions for the retarded have been closed and such patients are cared for in community group homes and by individual families.

Once a month, at facilities around the state, the DPW Medical Director conducted a meeting for state hospital administrators, their high level staff and several staff from DPW central office. Usually these meetings lasted several hours, and I was given the task of keeping minutes of the meeting. Usually I needed the better part of the next day to finalize the minutes. From this experience I learned much about the care of retarded persons.

I enjoyed working with Commissioner Morris Hursh who had been trained as a lawyer and was a classmate of former Governor Harold Le Vander at the University of Minnesota. Before he became Minnesota Welfare Commissioner, he spent many years as the CEO of Lutheran Services in Wisconsin. In his role as Commissioner he received many business letters, and it was part of my job to answer this correspondence. With the file and the letter attached on the top of each letter, he would indicate the type of response—business or personal— he would note to address it as Dear Mr. Smith or Dear Bill.

He was well liked and respected by all who came in contact with him. His favorite expression in advising on a problem was "use your best judgment". He possessed a wonderful sense of humor and enjoyed telling and hearing funny stories. I remember vividly the day several of us were in his office for an administrative meeting and he was interrupted by a telephone call. During a brief conversation with the person on the phone he was very polite. However, when the conversation ended, he slammed down the receiver and flatly said, "that son of a bitch".

When I made an application to take the State Bar Examination in June of 1960, I needed recommendations from three lawyers. I went to Morrie, as we called him, and asked if he would provide a recommendation. He said that he would be glad to provide one, "but I'm so busy would you please draft an affidavit in your behalf and I will sign it". I drafted a routine affidavit of recommendation and he signed it, but I was not present. Later that same summer I was in his office on an administrative matter and as I left, with a big smile on his face, he said, "Oh, Lew you certainly gave yourself a fine recommendation".

On June 14, 1960 I graduated from the William Mitchell College of Law. Commencement ceremonies took place at the College of St. Thomas Armory. Among the 68 in our graduating class were Charlie Gegen and Harry Schoen of Hastings. After the ceremony Marcella held a reception at our home that included Mother Linde and the Ruhrs. In the last week of July, I took the State Bar Exam, a three day ordeal, at the University of Minnesota Law School, which was not air–conditioned. With the very hot weather, T-shirts and shorts were the uniform of the day. The exam consisted of 24 essay questions on thirteen subjects. About 175 people sat for the exam, and oddly enough everyone passed the exam.

On October 4, 1960, with Marcella at my side, I was admitted to the Minnesota Bar at the State Capital Supreme Court Chambers alongside the same people with whom I sat for the exam. The morning ceremony was followed by a noon luncheon, sponsored by the Minnesota State Bar Association, at the downtown St. Paul Athletic Club. The day's festivities were heightened by the knowledge that Marcella was pregnant with a baby who would someday become Paul.

That same fall I started working for a non-profit organization, the Minnesota Prisoners Aid Society (later named Correctional Service of Minnesota) in downtown Minneapolis. I was initially hired as a social worker to help inmates who were being paroled from state correctional institutions in their efforts to return successfully to living in the community. My circuit of institutions included Stillwater Prison, St. Cloud Reformatory and the Woman's Prison at Shakopee. When I began visiting institutions and people found out that I was an attorney, my role quickly changed to providing legal advice and assistance to indigent inmates—which most of them were.

The director of the agency was Allan Hubanks. He came originally from Milwaukee, Wisconsin and had many years of correctional experiences. I learned many of the finer points of corrections and prisons from him. There were many impressive people on the agency's board of directors. To mention a few, it included James Otis, Minnesota Supreme Court Justice, Theodore Knudsen, Hennepin County District Court, Ben Berger, a prominent Minneapolis businessman, Rhoda Lund, an important member of the Minnesota Republican Party, and Geri Joseph, a top level Minnesota Democrat.

At that time, inmates who had been convicted and sentenced did not enjoy the benefit of an assigned public defender at the appellate level. Over the years, about 95 percent of all people convicted of a felony had entered a guilty plea. In the case of a guilty plea, the tedious process of a trial is avoided. In retrospect, many felons regretted having entered a guilty plea and not undergoing a trial. It was also true that these inmates who had plead guilty were less likely to have their conviction reversed on appeal. In spite of this fact my clients wanted to have a review of the convictions, even if their chance of winning an appeal was minimal.

Besides criminal cases, I handled divorce cases when the spouse lived in Hennepin County. I only took cases in which the marriage was dead and both parties wanted a divorce. To a lesser extent, I gave advice on other civil legal problems such as personal property and probate. My schedule included one day a week at Stillwater Prison, and one day every other week at the St. Cloud Reformatory. From time to time I visited the Shakopee facility and the Hennepin County Workhouse.

During my time there, I took an appeal to the Minnesota Supreme Court. A married couple, Raymond and Margaret Louise Jones were convicted of an armed robbery in Lake County. The facts showed that Margaret did not commit the robbery. With the help of C. Paul Jones, a Minneapolis criminal attorney, I perfected an appeal. Evidently the names of the Jones involved became confusing to a member of the Court. Besides the two defendants and my co-counsel C. Paul Jones, the Lake County Attorney was named Emmett Jones. During the course of the oral argument before the seven member court, a justice stopped me with the question, "Which Jones are you talking about?" The four people with the last name of Jones was too much for him to follow. The Supreme Court reversed Margaret's conviction.

From the fall of 1960 until April 1966, in the employ of Correctional Service, I dealt with many interesting and challenging clients. I had a front row seat in witnessing second-hand the numerous crimes and shortcomings of my clients. It also presented me with an opportunity to meet a diverse number of lawyers, judges, and administrators.

How I Got The Name Lew

From the earliest time I can remember my nickname was Louie. In my daily rounds in Cyrus at school, on the playground, and in the pool hall, it was Louie. The only exceptions were the teachers, and my dear mother, all of whom called me Llewellyn. My dad always called me Louie. So, when I left Cyrus for the Air Force in 1946, Louie was the name that followed me.

After I had worked for six months as both lawyer and social worker for Correctional Service in Minneapolis in 1961, the Director, Allan Hubanks, asked me, "Have you ever thought of changing your name to Lew?" I replied "No" and wondered why he asked me that question. His direct answer was that he believed the name Louie brought to mind the personage of a gangster, a confident man or a low-life. Since I was now a professional person, I bought the idea of changing my name to Lew. So it has been Lew ever since that day.

BACK TO THE DEPARTMENT OF PUBLIC WELFARE

In the spring of 1966 I had reached the point in my professional career where a change of jobs would be beneficial. Since I had earned my Masters Degree in Social Work and previously worked at the DPW in St. Paul, it was no problem to rejoin there during a time when professional workers were at a premium. I was placed in the Child Welfare Division as a consultant to private foster care and adoption agencies. On my first day back, I ran into Commissioner Hursh, who said, with a big smile on his face, "glad to have you back with us again, Lew".

The Child Welfare Division was directed by a capable and experienced man Web Martin. His approach to child welfare was liberal and progressive. Sometimes he reminded me of a latter-day Hippie. With his ready smile and good sense of humor, Web and I enjoyed a positive working relationship. His associate director Eli Lipschultz knew his business, but also demonstrated an explosive temper at times, On several occasions, Eli And I nearly got into a shouting match over our work, but we always managed to return to a cordial relationship.

I was assigned to act as a liaison between the department and private child welfare agencies such as Lutheran Social

Services, Catholic Charities, Jewish Family Service and Children's Home Society. Our involvement included issuing an annual license allowing them to provide adoptive and foster care services. It was my responsibility to visit these agencies on a regular basis to make certain that they were meeting all of the license requirements. It was my job to make arrangements for the quarterly business meetings of all of the agency directors. All the directors were highly motivated and conscientious. Because of this experience, I found a lifelong interest in subsidized adoptions and the reunion of adult adopted persons with their birth parents.

The success of my work with private agencies led to my promotion in mid 1968 to Statewide Supervisor of Adoptions and Foster Care. My administrative framework included supervising the overall program as well as eight professional social workers and five clerical staff. This professional staff provided direct services to Minnesota's 87 county welfare departments. To my good fortune, my staff, both professional and clerical, were hardworking and cooperative. Because our services were statewide, I had the opportunity to work with and get acquainted with child welfare workers all over Minnesota. In my entire professional career as a social worker, the areas of foster care and adoptions were my favorite. Looking back, I regret not staying in the child welfare field.

Because of my legal training, in late 1970 I was offered the position of Public Welfare's Chief Appeals Referee. My assistant, Jim Bares, was a very talented lawyer. Fundamentally, the position consisted of our hearing appeals in the areas of Aid to Dependent Children, Medical Assistance, and general relief recipients who were being denied benefits from county departments. Our jurisdiction was statewide, which meant that we heard appeals from Baudette to Austin. The average hearing included the welfare client (appellant) and a representative from the county welfare department. Usually the clients did not have legal representation, but the county welfare department was represented by their county attorney. Due to this imbalance, sometimes as hearing officers we had to protect the client's interests. The usual hearing lasted about an hour, before we would take the case under advisement and issue a written decision about three weeks later. By law we sat in the place of the Commissioner and he had to counter-sign all decisions. Commissioner Hursh, in all the cases, revised the language in only one case. Jim Bares and I reversed 70 percent of all appeals in favor of the client. After a while we were unpopular in the counties that we ruled against.

One case that I will never forget produced many newspaper articles and some editorials. The facts were uncomplicated. It happened that a single mother, Christine Frank, with two minor children applied for the program Aid to Families with Dependent Children (AFDC) in Blue Earth County, Mankato. She resided in a commune with several adults and their children. The County Welfare Department denied her application on the basis that she was not in a normal family living arrangement and that her present environment was detrimental to her children. There was no evidence showing that her children were abused or neglected. On the contrary, it was established that her children were well nurtured.

The appeal hearing was held in Mankato. Representing the County Welfare Department, the Blue Earth County Attorney's Office sent their top litigator, James C. Harten, who is now a member of the Minnesota Court of Appeals, He argued vociferously that the denial of AFDC benefits was proper. One of the main implications of his argument was that the mother and children were living in an immoral situation. The federal and Minnesota laws and regulations left no doubt about the fact that Christine and her children were clearly eligible for the program. After hearing the facts of the case, I reversed the denial of the county agency, with the full support of Commissioner Hursh. Upon the release of our decision, Blue Earth embarked on an aggressive publicity campaign in an attempt to turn public opinion against us. This generated many news stories—both pro and con. The Commissioner stood firmly by the decision, and, in a matter of a few weeks, the story was history.

MINNESOTA ADULT CORRECTIONS
COMMISSION (PAROLE BOARD)

During the time I provided legal services to the indigent at several Minnesota correctional institutions, I was always impressed by the activities of the parole board. Before Minnesota switched to determinate sentencing law, in 1982, the parole board held vast powers of discretion under the indeterminate sentencing structure. Offenders were given indeterminate sentences, and the parole board decided how long an inmate should be incarcerated and when a person should be paroled.

In the fall of 1971, the then-Chairman of the Parole Board, Ted Telander, retired, thereby creating a vacancy. I applied for the position of Chairman and was hired. David Fogel, the newly appointed Commissioner of Corrections, and Howard Costello, his deputy, made the appointment. In addition to obtaining recommendations from my former supervisors, I had to be cleared by the Minnesota Bureau of Criminal Apprehension.

The board consisted of my position as the full-time chairman and four part-time members, who were appointed to four-year terms by the Governor. When I assumed the chair, the other members of the Board constituted a rather diverse group. They were as follows: *Ben Berger,* a Jewish

Minneapolis business man who owned a string of movie theatres and was the original owner of the Minneapolis Lakers professional basketball team; *Ralph Tahash* who had worked in corrections for many years and was the retired warden of Stillwater Prison. While working as a federal prison employee in New Mexico, he had shot and killed an inmate in a prison riot. *Howard Rundquist,* also retired, was a former high school teacher who owned a grocery store in Willmar. *Wilford Antell,* a Native American, with advanced degrees in education, held a high position in the Minnesota Department of Education.

Most of the hearings were held with the three-member panels except those inmates who were serving a life sentence, in which the full board of five members was legally required to participate. Before a lifer could be paroled, the decision had to be unanimous. The vast majority of the three panel decisions were unanimous with the rest, of course, governed by a 2 to 1 decision. As chairman, my challenge was to maintain a high level of consistency and fairness in all decisions despite the composition of the panels being different nearly every day. All of the hearings were held at the adult correctional institutions in which the offenders were incarcerated.

Even with intelligent, mature and seasoned board members, it didn't take me very long to discover that there are many widely varied opinions of what constitutes the seriousness of a given crime and how much time a person should serve in prison as punishment. There was, of course, always a distinction between crimes against people and crimes against property. Fortunately, the final decision was generally based upon a compromise of thoughts and ideas. If a member held out against the other two members, a minority vote came about. By law, we were not obligated to maintain written minutes in denial or in support of our decisions, but, for the most part, our minutes offered an explanation of our rationale in reaching a particular decision.

Shortly after I took office, a real controversy arose when Commissioner Fogel, through the media, advocated that Ralph Tahash, Howard Rundquist and Ben Berger should resign from the board because they were all over the age of 65. Thankfully, Commissioner Fogel did not involve me in this process and these men fully understood that I had no part in this movement. All of them stood firm and did not give in to his demands. My first few months on the job were further complicated by an allegation that I was a puppet of Commissioner Fogel. The truth was that he never gave me any instructions regarding the cases except, in one instance, when he told me that he hoped the board would make a decision favoring the release of an inmate.

In the early 1970s the public was more aware of and was disturbed by issues of crime and punishment more than they are nowadays. This attitude was spawned by the Attica Prison riots in New York and the general unrest caused by the Vietnam War. There were news stories and editorials that stated that our decisions were too liberal and others accusing the parole board of being too conservative. Following the parole of a certain offender from Stillwater Prison, Governor Wendell Anderson invited us to the Governor's mansion for lunch to discuss our decision. In spite of the Governor's politeness and an elegant meal, the members were more than capable of justifying their decision. Ben Berger summed it up best when he said, "Governor, we take calculated risks, that's our legal responsibility."

During my tenure, some significant changes in the board membership took place. *Annette Whiting,* appointed by Governor Anderson, was the first woman ever to be appointed to the board. She was a University of Minnesota graduate, a business woman, a resident of Owatonna, a board member of Correctional Services of Minnesota and a Republican activist. At the hearings, profanity and obscene remarks in the presence of a woman diminished nearly to nothing. Annette had the rare ability to be tough with offenders when necessary and warm and understanding to other inmates as appropriate.

Another first was the appointment of two African-American members. *Charles Poe,* a lawyer and former Navy pilot, who was bound to a wheel chair because of polio he had contracted while in the military. His full-time job was as the executive director for a non-profit agency to assist African-American business people. He soon resigned to move to another state for employment reasons. After Charles Poe left the board, another African-American, *Richard Sessions,* a former executive with the Minnesota Department of Commerce, replaced him. Of all of the board members I worked with, he was by far the most conservative. In contrast to other board members, he believed that offenders should serve much longer sentences. As a result, when Richard served on a panel, he held the minority opinion in a high number of split votes.

Although I could write at length about the various personalities and decisions of the board, the combination of Linde, Tahash and Rundquist produced the most memorable situations. The offender would personally appear with a caseworker for his or her hearing. Before the hearing, each board member reviewed a document that described the individual's prior history and summarized the details of the current offense. Each of us would ask questions and offer commentary after the interview was conducted, the offender would be excused so the board could make a decision to either extend time in confinement or grant a parole.

When Ralph Tahash, the former warden, asked questions or offered commentary, he would often review the details of the crime in a harsh and unforgiving manner, often mixed with profanity. To say the least, the offender would be painfully reminded of the crime and often feel humiliated. On the other hand, Howard Rundquist, a former high school teacher, was warm and almost neighborly in his approach to inmates. He would ask personal questions about the offender's family and how things were going in confinement. When the offender left the room to permit the board to make a decision, Tahash and Rundquist would both distinctly change their tunes. Rundquist, the soft-hearted would turn tough and throw the proverbial book at the offender. Tahash, the hardcore, became tender-hearted and moderate, desiring to give the person a break. When the offender returned to the room for the decision, whatever it was, he or she had the clear impression that Tahash was the tough one and Rundquist was the one who gave the break.

In those situations where the members took opposing sides in a case, I tried to find middle ground, or I would side with the more liberal position. Many of the offenders we dealt with struggled with alcoholism. When granting parole to an alcoholic, Ben Berger often gave these words of advise: "When you go into a bar with the temptation to drink, count to ten first." We all could envision this person sitting on a bar stool and counting to ten before ordering a drink.

THE MINNESOTA
CORRECTIONS BOARD

In 1973 there was a certain amount of public dissatisfaction with a part-time parole board, and the movement was towards a full-time parole board. In that same year, Commissioner Fogel resigned and his post was assumed by Commissioner Kenneth Schoen. Along with Governor Anderson, the new Commissioner, the Legislature, and the State District Court Judges pushed for a full-time board. Besides the push to eliminate the older members of the board, a consensus was forming that change was needed.

The Minnesota legislature passed a law signed by Governor Anderson that created the Minnesota Corrections Board effective January 1, 1974. The chairman was to be appointed by the Commissioner of Corrections and the other five members were to be appointed by the Governor. That summer, Commissioner Schoen spoke publicly and to me personally that I would be appointed as the new chairman. Sometime in the early fall he changed his mind and designated Dick Mulcrone, a corrections supervisor in Scott County, to be the new chairman. Besides being a correctional professional, Mulcrone enjoyed a close connection with Governor Anderson. While I was disappointed that the position did not come to me, both Mulcrone and Schoen wanted me to be the new administrator of the board, a position which I accepted. The new board consisted of the following persons, none of whom had any parole experience. They were: *Les Melchert,* former Sheriff of Carver County; *P. Kenneth Peterson,* former Mayor of Minneapolis; *Les Green,* an ex-offender and former staff member at St. Cloud State University; and *Jane Belau,* a politically active Republican from Rochester. The legislation also provided that, as administrator, I could serve as a substitute board member when a regular member was on vacation or out ill. Since none of the members had any prior experience in parole work, my role as administrator and substitute turned into that of a mentor.

The new board developed some new guidelines, but its overall approach and decision-making did not deviate to any great extent from the old board. Dick Mulcrone turned to be a strong and decisive leader. When he was at a hearing or at an administrative meeting, he took full control, which everyone readily accepted. He served as chairman until 1979, when he left to joint the Federal Parole Board. He was replaced by Les Green. Jane Belau left and was replaced by *Dorothy Skweria.* Others who came on later were *Ron Byrnes,* a Minneapolis social worker; *Dick Alstad,* the former Chief of Police of Edina; *Jim Bruton,* a former correctional supervisor and NFL Placekicker from Ramsey County; and *Henry Green Crow,* a Native American and former schoolteacher.

Besides my new job as MCB Administrator, I was given the responsibility of developing a parole system for juvenile offenders at the institutions of Sauk Centre and Red Wing. When the MCB was created in 1974, the legislative also mandated that the parole and detention of juveniles be decided by administrators and staff of the institutions where the juvenile was confined. Juvenile paroles were determined by panels of three members at each institution. In addition to my frequent trips to adult correctional institutions, I also made regular visits to Sauk Centre and Red Wing.

At one point in my position as Executive Director of Juvenile Releases, Assistant Commissioner Orville Pung asked me to perform a user survey of juveniles confined at Sauk Centre and Red Wing. The final results were not unexpected and proved to be useful for planning purposes. Each survey had a blank space for any personal observations. The one comment that I will always remember was one by a young man at Sauk Centre who summed up his survey by writing, "this place stinks."

I can honestly report that I truly enjoyed working with each of the various board members from 1971 to 1982 and their different ideologies and personalities. While we sometimes disagreed about individual case dispositions and our approach to dispensing justice, any differences we had were professional and intellectual, never personal. Once at Stillwater that included Sheriff Melchert and two other members who got into a hearted discussion over the disposition of a case. The Sheriff asked me for my opinion, which differed with the other two panel members. After the decision was made, Melchert came up to me and whispered in my ear, "you know more about this business than the whole board put together."

THE MCB IS ABOLISHED

In the spring of 1982 the legislature passed a bill that was signed into law by Governor Quie, abolishing the MCB. It meant that Minnesota no longer had an indeterminate sentence law. Beginning July 1, 1982, criminal sentences were set by the District Court where the offender was convicted. The new law essentially said that an offender had to serve two thirds of the given sentence before being placed in supervised release. The Commissioner of Corrections was given the authority to parole offenders who were serving a life term and to revoke the supervised release of persons who violated the terms of their release agreements.

The date of April 22, 1982 remains vivid in my mind. It was the day that Commissioner Young told me that I no longer had a job in the Central Office after July 1, 1982. Unfortunately, the new law made no provision for the relocation or employment of myself or other MCB members. It was true, however, that Commissioner Young had the legal discretion to place me in another position in the department, but for whatever reasons which he never told me why I had to move on. A couple of the MCB members were disappointed that Governor Quie did not provide suitable exit arrangements for them. Jim Bruton, then Chairman of the MCB, told me that when he was appointed by the Governor, he was assured that if the MCB went out of business, he would be offered other state employment. He never heard from the Governor's office.

I was in a tough spot without employment as Marcella, Paul and Sara were still dependent upon my financial support. Thankfully, my good friend Ted Spencer, the Department of Corrections Personnel Director at the time, was of great assistance and helped me locate a supervisor's position at Stillwater Prison. The job-finding process lasted several weeks before the Stillwater job became a reality. In the meantime I had applied for other county and state positions, but there were no openings. Commissioner Young contacted Attorney General Spannaus about a possible position in the attorney general's office, but was turned down.

GOING TO WORK AT
STILLWATER PRISON

On July 1, 1982 I began my official duties at Stillwater Prison with the civil service classification of corrections supervisor. Since I had participated in many parole board hearings there over the years, many of the staff were my friends and there was no strangeness in appearing on the scene. There is an expression in the game of baseball in which player is designated as a utility player. To use the analogy in my situation, many different tasks were assigned to me. Some of my significant assignments were: Chair-Program Review Team, Chair-Safety and Wellness Committee, Affirmative Action Officer, Inmate Claims Officer, Policy and Procedure Author, Chair-Classification Committee, Training Instructor for Sexual Harassment Matters and How To Be A Witness In A Civil Court Proceeding. In my nine years at Stillwater Prison, I was officed in the former Farm Managers Residence located about a half mile from the main prison. The building never held more than six staff members, and because of our location, we seldom saw the top administrators. In other words, we had a lot of privacy.

From June 1984 to June 1985 I went on special assignment to St. Paul Central Office to engage correctional institutions in the reduction of worker compensation claims. The job involved meeting with institution heads and sources that could alleviate the problem. When getting into this problem, it didn't take long to discover that employee accident prevention and their personal wellness were the keys to a reduction of accidents. My main focus was the promotion of safety in the workplace and employee wellness, which provided me with the most enjoyable time of my last years of employment. After several health fairs I organized, it was common for fellow employees to come up to me and tell me how much they enjoyed the fairs and the positive impact it had on their personal health.

One of my challenges was to stir up enough interest for employees to participate in health fairs. One of my fellow employees from the central office laughed when I invited him to attend our Stillwater Health Fair. He did not accept my invitation, and unfortunately within the next two years he died of lung cancer. It was always difficult to convince custody staff (prison guards) to attend our health fairs. To overcome this attitude, we dispatched two of our male prison nurses to go to work locations to take blood pressure readings. Surprisingly, the cooperation was nearly one hundred percent. In their rounds of testing, six employees were identified with high blood pressure readings and were advised to see their family physicians immediately. After these experiences, it sometimes made me wish I would had pursued a career in public health education.

In the spring of 1991, the Minnesota Legislature passed a law which gave me the opportunity to retire with paid-in-full health benefits and an excellent pension plan. At age 63, I was ready to retire. I will be forever grateful to Ted Spencer and Warden Erickson for giving me the opportunity to work at

Stillwater Prison. Finally, I must mention my association with Warden Erickson during my Stillwater years. Over my working years, I would rate Warden Erickson as one of the best supervisors. He was in the same league as Commissioner Hirsh.

From time to time, I gave personally guided tours of the prison to outside officials and sometimes to friends and relatives. At the completion of a tour, if the warden was available, I would always like to take these visitors into his office for an introduction. He always made them comfortable.

One visitor will always be remembered. I was escorting the Safety Director of the Bayport X-Cel Energy coal burning power plant. She happened to be very experienced and well educated. At the end of the tour we went to the warden's office for her introduction. As we talked, it turned out that she went to high school at New Richmond, Wisconsin when the warden was the high school principal. She was one of his students. It didn't take long for the two of them to pleasantly reminisce about those school years. As the discussion went on, the warden told about one of his students who sometimes presented discipline problems. He came up with the story about the time the same student was caught smoking in the boys bathroom perched up on a toilet stool in an individual stall. The safety director began to laugh almost uncontrollably and said, "I was married to that man—we were divorced years ago". To say the least the warden was completely surprised and we all had a good laugh.

RETIREMENT YEARS

On July 1, 1991, I retired from my employment at Stillwater Prison. Coffee and cake were served at my retirement party in the employee's dining room. It was heart-warming to see my friends and fellow employees. Warden Erickson, Commissioner Pung and Deputy Commissioner Howard Costello were present as were Marcella, Kay and Sara. Warden Erickson awarded the traditional gold watch and service plaque to me.

Marcella and I always liked the idea of "if you don't take advantage of traveling while in good health and otherwise able, the day will come when you can't travel because of illness or death." Following that principle, that same summer we went on a 17-day bus trip through the Canadian Rockies to Alaska. On the last day we flew from Anchorage back to Minneapolis. The highlight of the trip was touring Denali National Park, which is the size of the State of Massachusetts. The sight of Mount McKinley was breathtaking. We also had the chance to observe moose, mountain sheep and grizzly bears in the wild. The scenery in Canada and Alaska is spectacular. Since Rick became a flight attendant in 1976, Marcella and I took advantage of family pass privileges going on trips, sometimes taking Sara and Paul. We took trips to Boston, Philadelphia, New York, Los Angeles, Chicago, Nashville, Branson, Missouri, and, of course, San Francisco where Paul and Laurie live.

Our first two-week trip to Europe came about in 1985 when we traveled to Denmark, Norway and Sweden. The most exciting thing about this trip was meeting many of my cousins for the first time on Sogn Fjord near Balestrand, Norway. My relatives really rolled out the welcome mat for us. In 1987 we embarked an another two-week trip to Germany, Switzerland and Austria. The high points included cruising down the Rhine River, and sightseeing in Salzburg and Munich.

We experienced another pleasant two-week trip in 1993 when we traveled to Ireland, Scotland, Wales and England. Ireland was our favorite place. We especially enjoyed a tour of the Waterford Glass Factory and mixing with the local people. As in Scandinavia and Ireland, the local citizens were laid-back and friendly. We spent only a few days in London, but regretted that we couldn't have spent more time in this historic and vast city. The Scottish Highlands more than exceeded our expectations.

The grandfather of all our trips happened in the fall of 1994 when Marcella, Rick and I traveled to Zimbabwe. The flight from London to Harare was thirteen hours non-stop. We spent seventeen days with Paul and Laurie. Laurie was a member of faculty of the University of Zimbabwe Medical School, and Paul was a staff psychiatrist at a large public hospital. Paul took some time off for the four us to take a trip to the famous Hwange Park and Game Reserve. We identified about 30 kinds of wild game and birds. Unlike a zoo, where animals are confined and few in number, it was thrilling and amazing to see herds of elephants, zebra, giraffes, and antelopes. We spent the better part of a day observing one of the seven wonders of the world, Victoria Falls. The falls are one mile in width and have a drop of 350 feet. While in Victoria Falls, we spent an evening watching a performance of native singing and dancing. Afterwards we enjoyed an elegant dinner in a stylish tourist hotel dating back to colonial days. Marcella, Rick and I took an overnight train trip from Victoria Falls to a large nearby city, Bulowayo. From our sleeping compartment it was exciting to see the countryside in full moonlight. Bulowayo, originally built and founded by Cecil Rhodes, was modern with many interesting sights, including a trip to the Matopos Hills National Park. This park is unusual because of its memorial to a designer of colonialism, Cecil Rhodes, as well as its uneven stone formations. Poverty among the population was ever present in this third world country, and it was depressing to be around and see suffering people.

In the summer of 1997 we took a ten-day bus trip in the western United States to visit the National Parks of Roosevelt in North Dakota, Glacier and Yellowstone in Montana, Grand Tetons in Wyoming and Mount Rushmore in South Dakota. The weather was perfect and, of course, the scenery beautiful. That fall we took a bus trip to Branson, Missouri to see several musical shows. Andy Williams always had been a favorite of Marcella and his show was outstanding. Among other shows we liked the presentation of the Radio City Rockettes. Their beauty and precision dancing are something one rarely witnesses.

Our travels gave us many happy memories.

Out in the Community

COMMUNITY ACTIVITIES

Marcella always had a positive outlook on the best welfare and progress of Hastings and took an active part in many organizations. In the 1960s she was a member of the City of Hastings Planning Commission along with such people as Attorney Dave Tanner and Lu Stoffel, a former mayor of Hastings. The Planning Commission was advisory to the Hastings City Council in matters of residential ad commercial zoning, because Hastings was an ever growing and changing city, controversy was the order of the day. Also, in the 1960s a joint school board of St. Boniface and Guardian Angels Church Schools was established. Marcella was the first woman to become a member of this board. As a mother of school-aged children and a former hospital administrator, Marcella made a valuable contribution to the success of these schools.

In the late 1980s Marcella became a volunteer counselor for Birthright of Hastings. The main mission of this agency was to provide counseling and limited material support to unmarried teenage pregnant girls. Along with free pregnancy testing, the counselors helped these young women deal with a multitude of challenges and conflicts associated with an unwanted pregnancy. Because of her nurse's training and varied experiences, Marcella was very effective in helping these girls come to grips with their new situation. While the counseling was individualized, Birthright volunteers worked in pairs. She became good friends and worked frequently and women like Jan Shannon, Kathy Gahnz, and Kathy Casperson. Marcella's nursing background was utilized when she helped out the local American Red Cross blood drives. She was a regular volunteer for the local immunization clinic at Hastings High School, held monthly for infants and school children. This clinic was sponsored by the Hastings Women's Club. Marcella developed some nice friendships with the nurses and women who worked with her in this activity.

Always interested in the advancement of women's rights, Marcella became a charter member of the American Association of University Women, Hastings Chapter.

Church work was always a top priority for Marcella. Her activities included helping out at funeral luncheons, counting the Sunday offering on Mondays and helping patients at the Augustana Home attend Mass. Whenever a volunteer was needed, Marcella always responded to the recruitment requests favorably. While Marcella never carried her religious beliefs on her sleeve, she was firmly committed to her faith in God which was demonstrated by her regular attendance at mass and a weekly hour visitation and prayer at the Blessed Sacrament at St. Elizabeth Ann Seton Chapel.

Lew's Community Activities

During my younger, family years, the Boy Scout movement absorbed much of my interest. Beginning in the early 1960s I became cub master—a post I held for two years. The main focus of a cub master is to develop an ongoing relationship with the den mothers who held weekly meetings with a group of 8 to 10 boys. Marcella was an active den mother. A major event of the dens was a monthly Blue and Gold pot luck dinner, which was usually held in a church basement or VFW clubroom. After the pot luck meal, games were played and rousing songs were sung. I recall one Blue and Gold meal when Myra Swanson brought a large delicious wild rice and sausage hotdish (casserole outside of Minnesota). Several mothers brought the traditional pan of pork and beans. The boys got their fill of pork and beans, ignorant and unaware of the award-winning wild rice casserole. I guess I ate their share of wild rice.

In 1970 I became Scout Master of troop 503 for a term of two years. Being the head of a troop meant weekly meetings and monthly outings, sometimes including overnight camping. Also, every summer I spent a week with the troop at Tomahawk Scout Reservation near Rice Lake, Wisconsin. Our troop had an average membership of 25 boys. Overall, the boys were full of energy, but well-behaved and willing to work on the stepladder of their ranks, by earning merit

From left to right: Rick Linde, Jim McNeal, Eric Flom, Jim Sontag, Mark Rego, Dave Gunter, and Lew Linde, Scoutmaster.

badges and doing various projects. A Senior Patrol Leader was a valuable source of help at all meetings and activities. I know I am perhaps missing some boys, but I remember well Mark Rego and John and Gary Gunter. The highlight of this experience was when the following boys were awarded their Eagle badges at a ceremony: Dave Gunter, Mark Rego, Eric Flem, Jim Sontag, Rick Linde, and James McNeal.

As a college graduate with a teaching certificate in Social Studies and Speech, education had always been one of my big interests. Following this passion, I ran for the school board in 1964. I lost that election perhaps because I was not well known in Hastings. The idea of the school board did not leave me as I ran for the board in 1979 and was elected for a three-year term, after which I lost my bid for reelection.

In retrospect my short elected life on the board was caused largely by my outspokenness and failure to be diplomatic at times. I guess I thought I was back on the parole board speaking directly to prison inmates.

Part of my frustration as a board member was that at times when dealing with administrative actions my fellow members took a "me too" position and acted like honorary pall bearers. Overall, it must be said that Marcella and I had a deep respect for the Hastings Public School System. Our children did receive an excellent education.

My proudest activity began in 1969 when I helped organize Hastings Family Service. The following brief, written in May 2000, provides a good picture of HFS past and present:

HISTORY The origin of Hastings Family Services had a humble beginning. In the late 1960s Dawn Sheridan (Beedle) in her contacts with local elementary teachers became acutely aware of the fact that there were children coming to school who were inadequately clothed and undernourished. It was surmised that these children came from disadvantaged families. Dawn, in her own pioneer and innovative manner, enlisted the help of her neighbors and friends, particularly Mary Jean Engstrom and Virginia McHale, in gathering food and clothing which was initially in Dawn's basement and became the distribution center. Referrals for food and clothing mainly came from elementary teachers and principals. These basement efforts went on for several years. In 1969 Lew Linde joined the three ladies in many hours of deliberations to determine whether to develop and incorporate a formal agency which would encompass these helping functions.

On April 17, 1970, Hastings Family Service legally became a Minnesota non-profit corporation. The incorporators were Dawn Sheridan, Mary Jean Engstrom, Virginia McHale, and Lew Linde. These individuals served as the Board of Directors until about 1975 when the board was expanded. In the summer of 1970, store space was rented in a building on Ramsey Street, south of the Post Office. That particular building was demolished in about 1980, and the Hastings Senior Center is now located on the same land. Since then the agency has had several locations. The store was then and is now called the Clothes Closet and Food Shelf. Shortly thereafter, the agency started to receive monetary support from the United Way of Hastings along with clothing, food and money from the public.

These past thirty years reflect steady progress and growth in services. For the past fifteen years, the agency has been under the excellent leadership of the Executive Director, Janet Gratz.

Countless numbers of people, young and old, especially children, have benefited from the necessities of life and the reassuring help from our efficient staff. Mention must be made of the importance of the many volunteers and the generous gifts of time, talents, clothes, goods, food and money. HFS has become the kind and loving neighbor to the less fortunate. Goods and services are freely provided regardless of race, color, religion, sex, political beliefs or marital status.

Hastings Family Service has an honorable and respected past. The future is well established. The Scriptures state it best, "Whoever is kind to the poor lends to God, and will be repaid in full."—Proverbs 19:17

SOUTHERN MINNESOTA
REGIONAL SERVICES

Retirement without a plan of action can be uninteresting and dull. Because I never actively practiced law for long periods of time after finishing law school in 1960, there was always the temptation to allow my attorney license to lapse. Marcella always encouraged me to keep my license, which I did. To maintain it, I had to take annual continuing legal education classes, and pay an annual fee. I also kept my membership in the Minnesota State Bar Association. About a year before my retirement from the State of Minnesota in 1991, I decided that I wanted to do pro bono (voluntary services) in the area of family law. Not knowing exactly to begin, I contacted Nancy Kleeman of the MSBA. She put me in touch with Bruce Beneke, Executive Director of SMRLS in St. Paul. Although most of the cases were handed by their regular legal services staff, some of SMRLS's work was supplied by pro bono lawyers. There was always a long list of clients waiting for services. At that time there was an unusually high number of clients in Goodhue County (Red Wing) waiting for assistance. In late fall of 1991, I began to see clients in Red Wing. My home office was in the Minnesota Building in St. Paul, where I had the benefit of an office, secretarial services and a law library. I was pleasantly surrounded by 6 or 7 attorneys in the Family Law Unit. Gwen Werner, a well-experienced and seasoned family law lawyer became my mentor to help me in tough and unusual cases. Our unit met once a week over coffee, rolls and snacks. Besides problem-solving and exchanging ideas, we had many good laughs about ourselves, the profession and, good-naturedly, about some of our clients. Beverly Anderson, my first unit director, later became a Referee in the Ramsey County Family Court. Her successor was Susan Cochrane, who later became a Referee in the Hennepin County Family Court. James Street, a veteran legal services lawyer, succeeded Susan Cochrane and is still the family law unit director.

Early on, I had the privilege of working with some great lawyers who became my friends. Special mention must be made of a colleague, Mary Al Balber, a Native American. Mary Al and I covered Goodhue County together where we shared a variety of clients, I was always impressed by her natural beauty and legal brilliance. On our trips we had some pleasant luncheons at the St. James Hotel. Her sage advice and counsel on tough cases was always beneficial.

My trip to Red Wing ended in 1994 when Goodhue County was absorbed by the Winona SMRLS office. My volunteer work then took me to St. Paul on the average of three days per week. Due to Marcella's illness, I had to take a leave of absence in January 1997 until the spring of 1999 when I resumed my activities. When I took my shingle down in the summer of 2000, the entire SMRLS staff threw a surprise party to celebrate my 40th anniversary as a member of the Minnesota Bar.

During my time at SMRLS I exclusively dealt with no-fault divorce cases. It was fortunate that the vast majority of my referred cases were uncontested, which meant that the parties involved were generally non-adversarial. I was given the nickname of Dr. Default. While I don't know exactly why all of my clients were women, they represented a cross section of races and cultures in St. Paul. About one-half of my clients were Caucasian with the remainder being African-American, Hispanic, Native American, and Jewish. At the time of my departing in the fall of 2000, I had represented a total of 115 clients, much to my surprise, and a record for SMRLS volunteer lawyers.

Marriage problems cross all economic, racial and cultural lines. Sad to say, one-half of all our present-day marriages end in divorce. There are many reasons why marriages fail. From my limited experience, the major reasons were infidelity, money problems and substance abuse. Running through these cases was the underlying notion that if it doesn't work, get rid of it. Years ago people stayed in marriage. Through thick and thin. It would be easy for me to tell the tough luck stories of my clients, there experiences and our interactions. But, I am going to remain silent, because I do not want to violate the attorney-client relationship. At the end of every hearing when the divorce had been granted and we left the courtroom, consistently without reluctance, every client thanked me profusely for helping them get out of a "bad marriage". Occasionally, a client would give me a hug. To me, that expression of gratitude paid me well for my pro bono services.

Lew and Marcella Linde Family, 1972.

Family Stories

Thanks for the Memories

By Ken Linde

To try to highlight one or even a few of my fondest memories of growing up in the Linde family would be a difficult if not impossible task. My tribute to family life is the cumulative 50 year memory bank I have filled. I enjoyed a safe, healthy, loving and nurturing environment. Individual memories of great times celebrating birthdays, holidays, and big life events abound. Together those individual memories make up my lifetime thus far. It has been good—and certainly worth remembering.

For me, family life didn't start and then end at some time when I left the nest. It has continued to grow as we have grown older in age and somewhat apart in terms of miles and differing extended family situations. Our family has survived tragedy and heartache. We have also celebrated all the good things of life—marriages, births, adoptions, graduations, promotions, recognition. One fond story involves a bottle of whiskey. Dad had received a bottle of whiskey in the shape of W. C. Fields head. Upon bringing this gift home, he announced that he would not open it until some really big event came along. So, the bust of W. C. sat on the shelf for many years as if waiting for just the right "big event". Births came and went. Graduations came and went. Marriages came and went. One big event after another came and went. "Dad, when are we going to open that bottle of whiskey?" My guess is that it has long ago dried up—something that W. C. Fields himself apparently never did!

I made it through grade school, high school, college and, at least so far, the work world. Through each chapter of my growing up years, I have always known love and encouragement. I was given every opportunity to succeed—and to fail. **No** one did it for me, but everyone taught and encouraged me. I had grandparents who were a regular and vital part of my life. I had loving parents who went to the end with me and for me.

My memories tend to blur one to another. Though the circumstances may be different, all blend together because the root is the same—fun, laughter, sharing, celebration, and love. I am not a big fan of outwardly celebrating holidays and have made the mistake of being a bit too vocal about this. But, I do inwardly celebrate that we can be together. I particularly enjoyed this past Christmas when in my wife Carol's family and in the Linde family, we focused our giving on those less fortunate than us. We chose to give to those for whom life has not been so kind. In tears on Christmas Eve, we heard about others touched by our gifts. Christmas came alive in focusing on gift-giving to those outside our family. I know that Mom would have loved this Christmas. She, who by her selfless giving, taught us so much about reaching out beyond our own selves.

I have experienced many high points in my life. Being a father to incredible daughters has taught me to be sure to "walk the talk" because they are always watching. And though I know I tripped once in a while, I think I did alright in this. Being blessed with a second chance in marriage has taught me to be thankful. To be loved as I am loved is truly an awesome sense of the fullness of life. To step into a young adult's life as her mother's husband and her stepfather is a learning experience as we each try to get to know one another. And then when you feel like you're more than just accepted, it is a humbling experience. When a father gazes upon his daughter holding her newborn son it is perhaps the most "heavenly like" experience of all. To try to put into words the feelings and senses that are affected would be futile. It will perhaps only be topped by hearing him call me Grandpa!

And so, my fondest memory of life with the Lindes is really a dynamic and ongoing one. It started and has yet to end. I'm grateful for a loving family. I miss Mom and often wish she were still here celebrating life with us. But I also know she is in a far better place—probably getting the house ready for us. I do know they love her there—just as we do here. Thanks for the memories.

THE SURPRISE VISIT

by Rick Linde

The topic of adoption had come up several times at the Linde household discussed at the dinner table, in the living room after Sunday Mass and by Mom and Dad in their private conversations after supper. Of course, we kids also put our own two cents worth in every now and then. After all, what kid wouldn't want a cute and cuddly little baby brother or sister to play with.

It was in the mid and late sixties that Dad worked as an administrator for the Child Adoption and Foster Care Services Department for the State of Minnesota. You can understand why the subject of adoption was near and dear to his heart. Dad was moved by the need for children to have a safe, secure and loving home to grow up in. As Mom and Dad were both in their early forties, the possibility of having another child was an unlikely and somewhat scary option for them. The concept of adoption seemed a realistic and viable alternative at the time.

All that consideration changed abruptly in the early months of 1969. At Christmas time, Mom was sick with what she thought was probably the infamous Hong Kong Flu. She had bouts of lightheartedness, stomach upset, nausea, and some dizziness and vomiting. After nearly a month of these symptoms, Mom finally decided to make an appointment at the clinic in Red Wing to determine what the problem was. A winter ice and snow storm hit the day of the appointment and thankfully (and fatefully) Dad took the day off to accompany her to the clinic. After a thorough examination and full morning of tests, Mom was diagnosed with PREGNANCY. It was fortunate Dad was with her as I don't think Mom could have made it home alone considering the shock factor and weather situation.

I will never forget coming home from school that cold and snowy January day and seeing Mom sitting at the kitchen table with a somewhat stunned and somber gaze.

I immediately remembered the appointment and thought the worst. I was somewhat puzzled by the fact that Dad was leaning against the stove with a smirkish grin on his face. When I had the guts to ask what was going on, Mom burst into tears and blurted out the words she still couldn't believe. "I'm pregnant!!!!" What a shock. Those shock waves rippled throughout our household for months and subsided somewhat as the August due date approached. I distinctly remember Mom waking me up in the wee hours of the morning to tell me she was going to the hospital. She was dressed in that all too familiar navy blue and daisy print maternity shift. Still half asleep I innocently asked why. "I'm going to have a baby" was her matter of fact response. So on August 5, 1969 (while men were on the moon and the 60s were drawing to a close) little Sara Jennifer Linde entered the world and ours. What some would consider a "menopausal mistake" was for all of us a memorable and blessed event.

With four siblings, three of whom were well into their teens, Sara grew up hearing of our school adventures, wedding plans, the Viet Nam War and the Nixon resignation. No wonder she never talked baby talk. Being 15 at the time, I especially remember forfeiting several weekend nights to baby-sit, bathe, change, feed and sing endless verses of "Raindrops Keep Falling On My Head" until Sara finally went to sleep. In the summer time I would fill the pool or set the lawn sprinkler so Sara and her neighborhood friends could splash and play. I would even take her for rides on the Sno Jet in our yard in the winter. And the day 1 left for college. Sara was just three years old. As Mom helped Dad and I finish packing the car, Sara ran down the driveway crying and screaming "Ricky don't go, Ricky don't go!!" Although my four years at college separated us somewhat, it was always a highlight coming home and having Sara greet me with a hug. When home one year during break I had laid down on the couch (as usual) after a hefty Thanksgiving dinner. Sara ran over and jumped up to lay on my back. At that I let out a large burp to which she replied, "oh yuk, you have turkey breath."

Sara is all grown up now. I have watched her play in golf tournies, witnessed three graduations and helped her move into her first apartment to start her first teaching job. I was elated to have her move to the Twin Cities to start a new career in Counseling and to have helped her buy her first home. And now her camaraderie and friendship is a constant reminder of the gift and blessing it is to have her in my life and in our family. Although there are countless more stories to relate and many family memories I hold dear, I still think the addition of Sara to our family stands out as the most prolific and enduring of all. It changed the complexion of our family forever.

KAY'S REFLECTIONS

by Kay Linde Talafous

When I think about growing up in our family I think of the constant support I received. Mom and Dad were very actively involved in all of our activities. You name it, they were there. PTA, Girl Scouts, Boy Scouts, all of our school and extracurricular functions, athletic events, music lessons, etc. I must admit that I just thought this was normal family life. I took it all for granted and didn't really fully realize the commitment and love that went into being such supportive, wonderful parents until I became a parent myself. The most important aspect of that support and love was not the physical or the financial but rather the emotional.

I know I always felt that my parents would be there for us no matter what happened. And they were. From the little everyday happenings to the major crises in our lives, they were there with loving open arms, a shoulder to cry on, and advice if needed and wanted. Again, I took this for granted and naively assumed everyone was raised in such a loving, open atmosphere. As I ventured out into the world, first in college and then as a young married woman and later on as a young mom, I began to realize how wonderful it was to have that constant attention and support and also that many of the people I met along the way did not necessarily have the same experience.

I am certain that it wasn't always easy. I have come to know as a parent myself that you need to be ready for just about anything in life. We challenged often and much. But we always knew that the love and concern was there no matter what the situation.

I remember my wonderful mom as being a very strong woman and a very loving and giving person. No questions asked. She would do without to make sure we had what we needed physically and emotionally. She raised me to be a strong independent woman as well and I now see that strength in my own daughter and granddaughter. I miss her greatly.

I was married for almost 22 years and most of those years were wonderful. During the time of my separation and divorce my family was behind me with care, concern and support always. They have always been there for my children as well. My daughter Amanda Marie Talafous was born on April 14, 1979 and my son Peter Dean Talafous was born October 15, 1980. My mom came to New York after each birth to love up her grandchildren and help me out. My own granddaughter Ella Julia Talafous was born on September 3, 2000. 1 had the privilege of being there with Amanda for the birth and I get to see Ella and love her up every day! I know that my mom would have loved to have been here physically for Ella but her love comes down from heaven daily in so many wonderful ways. My children and grandchild are the most important things in the world to me. That is the way I felt growing up and I know they feel that same love and commitment. I am so thankful for the family support we have from my brothers Ken, Rick and Paul and my sister Sara and their families as well.

They say as you age you become your parent or parents. If it is a true compliment, I consider that a huge compliment.

NEAR-DEATH AT ITASCA STATE PARK

By Paul Linde

It depends on whether you're the type of person who sees the glass as half full or half empty. These days I prefer to view that glass as three-quarters full because a positive spin might take you places while doom and gloom will only take you down.

If one believes in those psychological theories that emphasize birth order, then you'd probably see me as having the potential for being one pretty mixed-up kid. And on that question, the jury is still out. You see, I was born as the baby of the family, a mere pup in comparison to Ken, Kay, and Rick a role that I savored for many years. Then I was virtually an only child for a couple more. And then I shared the stage with baby Sara, all of a sudden becoming an older brother for another ten years or so. The only sibling role I never played (deep sigh of relief) was the middle kid. Because I've been trained as a psychiatrist and tossed tens of thousands of dollars toward the pursuit of sanity via psychotherapy, I'm entitled to make up whatever cockamamie theory I want. So there!

I can only speculate that I wasn't too emotionally traumatized by nearly getting gassed to death up at Itasca State Park Resort. But judging by my resultant proclivity for ritualistic rocking and barricading myself in my room with my crib, I wouldn't be so sure. Though Mom always said it was a thyroid condition that caused my premature corpulence, could just as easily conjure up some sort of fancy psychological explanation for my enthusiastic overeating, which eventually necessitated a trip to Weight Watchers. If only I could have scored some pharmaceutical- grade speed from one of those maniacal "fat" doctors. Then I'd have the potential for being really screwed up and maybe even a speed junkie.

Except for Rick's "Indian sunburns" and "knobbies", I'm sure I was pretty well spoiled by Ken, Kay, and Rick.

I don't think I became an annoyance or borderline embarrassment until they were all well confined in the shackles of adolescence. And then I had the opportunity to view firsthand the effects of raging teen hormones. I also witnessed some fascinating socio-cultural phenomena, namely the pursuit of fashionably straight hair by virtue of donning a stretchy nylon stocking for a sleeping cap (Rick) and taking those curly locks to the ironing board (Kay). In addition, like any little kid, I hated hearing arguments so I received an early crash course on the finer points of mediation. Blessed be the peacemakers.

By the time Ken, Kay, and Rick left for college one-by-one, I was so lonely on Sunday nights I wanted to cry. So much for me being able to enjoy the role of the only child. I much preferred the chaos and hubbub of a full house at 1610 Tyler Street to the quietness of a Sunday evening and undone homework. I wanted nothing more than to hang out and do things with them, even if that meant memorizing the Guinness Book of World Records or the World Almanac so I could beat them at trivia. I suppose I could view myself as "worldly" at a young age,

When my 44-year-old mother's case of the flu turned into

a full-fledged "Urfnah", my feelings were mixed. While I saw the prospect of a younger sibling as threatening to my role as the baby in the family, I also viewed "Luella" as someone who could take over some of my household chores in a few years. And, of course, on a certain level, I welcomed God's gift of life to our family and the chance to be a big brother. While Mom endured labor and delivery in August of 1969 and Dad smoked cigarettes, pacing in the hospital waiting room, I whiled away the day at Como Park Zoo with the cousins. It was truly exciting when Mom and Sara came home.

After surviving overnight feeds and every two-hour diaper changes of Jacob and Sam as an "older parent", I can now fully appreciate how much work it was for Marcella and Lew to be parents to not just a thriving newborn, but also three teenagers and an eight-year-old boy.

Sara was a fun and thrilling baby and toddler—"Boodie Sinner"—and we all enjoyed taking care of her. As Ken, Kay, and Rick went off to college to tackle the real world, I tried to be as benign and benevolent an older brother as I could be to Sara. Mom and Dad and Sara and I did enjoy a lot of trips together, the most memorable the one to my future home city of San Francisco, where I experienced my first full-fledged Hare Krishna rush at Fisherman's Wharf. As an emergency psychiatrist nowadays, I still find the city full of interesting characters. But, despite fun trips and family time together, I'm sure Sara still experienced some distancing from me as I slouched and stumbled into the confusion that is adolescence.

But as Sara and I grow older, we become closer existentially, not just nearer in age. I guess those eight-and-a-half years don't mean as much when the former babies of the family reach the milestones of forty and thirty years of age. And as I struggle with the demands of career and family, I feel a greater closeness with my older siblings—"Flower Power" children turned into Gray Panthers, on the brink of AARP eligibility. Take no offense, Ken, Kay, and Rick, because, just like thirty years ago, I am right behind you and you are just ahead of me.

Don't blow my Social Security before I get there.

BEING THE YOUNGEST

By Sara J. Linde

In sitting down to write about a memory from my childhood, a number of thoughts raced through my mind-thoughts that caused some smiles, tears, and even some out-loud laughs. I thought a lot about the 'Tyler Street House' era-walking (or begging Dad for a ride) down to Kennedy Elementary to go skating at the city-flooded ice rink or sledding down the BIG HILL, 'weighing in' at the blue and green flowered love seat with Paul in order to transform the living room into a wrestling arena, and riding my bike to the creamery to buy milk for Mom (and probably some candy for myself). Most of all, I remember growing up in a supportive household that stressed the importance of being good to one another, maintaining strong family ties, holding steadfast in our faith, and helping others.

I never knew our house at 1610 Tyler Street without the 'family room'. I heard a lot of stories about how crowded the house was before the addition, but many of my memories came from time spent in the western-most part of the house. As a toddler, my most (in)famous feat took place after many of my baths, when I streaked through the family room yelling "Booty Sinner" (in more understandable English: 'Beauty

Winner'), much to the chagrin of my older siblings who often had company over to watch television. After being herded back to the bathroom to get my pajamas on, I would get to return to the family room and be the center of attention or at least that's how I saw it, I'm not sure if that's how my brothers and sisters viewed the situation.

The family room served as our dining room as well, and I remember birthday parties and Thanksgiving and Christmas dinners taking place with all three leaves in the table. When the table wasn't needed for large gatherings, it served its purpose well for me to put my books on it when I returned home from school every day. The other family room furniture proved to be very comfortable and functional; Mom always sat in her chair with the coffee-cup-ring-stained TV tray next to it, and when we had guests, like the time when Paul brought Linda Schams home to meet us (and I giggled the whole time), the love seat was just perfect for two.

The family room couch, which is now housed in the 'Seventh Street House' basement, held many functions in the Linde household. Not only did it serve to seat a great number of family members and guests, it was the place where I fell asleep each night. Like clockwork, I would insist on watching my usual shows, nodding off to sleep, and having Dad carry me (or later on, walk me) back to my room. Boy, did I have him trained. I also remember lying on that couch whenever I was sick. We were lucky, because we didn't have to stay in our beds when we were sick. Mom would put a sheet and blanket down on the couch, and I would get to carry my pillow out to lie with a TV tray next to me that always had a glass of 7-UP and some saltines on it. Those were the days before remote controls, so Mom would sit near me (in her chair with her TV tray next to it, of course) and turn the channels to my liking. I would lie on the couch staring up at the wall where the high school graduation pictures of the older kids hung, dreaming of the time when my picture, too, would be hanging near theirs.

When my parents decided to move from the 'Tyler Street House', I had just finished ninth grade. I was no longer streaking through the house after bathtime or having Dad carry me to bed after falling asleep on the couch, but I did spend a lot of time in the family room watching the newly installed cable television. I also had gotten into the habit of sitting on the couch with a TV tray to do my homework, sometimes right after school, but usually later in the evening while watching shows like "Dallas" and "Love Boat", or videos on MTV. Many summer afternoons were spent on the floor with friends playing board games when the weather was too hot and we wanted to take full advantage of the air conditioning.

I was fortunate to have many of the same amenities at the 'Seventh Street House', and, although I missed the familiarity of the old house, I really enjoyed the excitement of moving into the new house. The family room furniture became 'den' furniture when we first moved, and later became 'basement' furniture, where it currently resides. For many of this piece's readers, you will probably notice a very distinct omission from my recollections . . . and that is the memory of the old green chair that once held great respect in the family room as Dad's chair. It lived for a while in some of Paul's post-high school and post-college homes—for now, let's just say that it probably isn't housed next to Archie Bunker's in the Smithsonian!